Simon was
She should

That way, he'd never know she'd been there. But she couldn't leave a sleeping man and his house to the mercy of a possible intruder.

Before she could utter the cool words she'd planned or change her mind about saying anything at all and run for her life, she felt her arm seized in a viselike grip. The next moment, she was yanked sideways, landing in a sprawled heap on the bed—literally on top of Simon Devlin!

His strong arms closed around her and she heard his voice, very soft. ''Well, I wasn't expecting this.''

Tanya panicked. ''Simon, let me go!''

Instead, he gripped her more tightly. ''Never look a gift horse in the mouth, they say,'' he drawled. Then he pressed his mouth to hers.

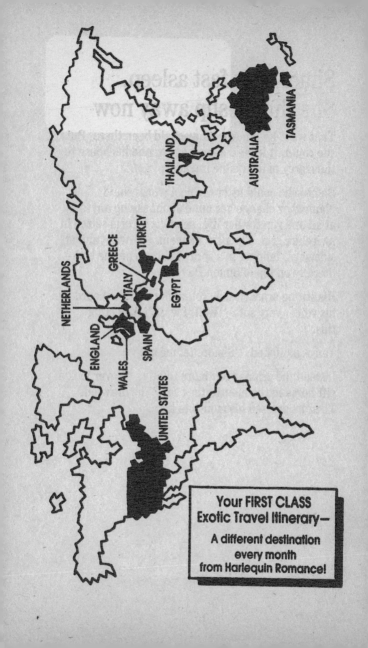

NETHERLANDS
ENGLAND
WALES
GREECE
ITALY
SPAIN
TURKEY
EGYPT
THAILAND
AUSTRALIA
TASMANIA
UNITED STATES

Your FIRST CLASS
Exotic Travel Itinerary—

A different destination
every month
from Harlequin Romance!

FAIR
TRIAL
Elizabeth Duke

Harlequin Books

TORONTO • NEW YORK • LONDON
AMSTERDAM • PARIS • SYDNEY • HAMBURG
STOCKHOLM • ATHENS • TOKYO • MILAN

Original hardcover edition published in 1990
by Mills & Boon Limited

ISBN 0-373-03110-6

Harlequin Romance first edition March 1991

FAIR TRIAL

CHAPTER ONE

'YOU'RE spending the weekend with *Simon Devlin*? Out in the *bush*?' Tanya's best friend and flatmate Ellie, a solicitor like herself, gave a low whistle. 'Half your luck!'

'You make it sound as if we're going to be camping out under the mulgas and living on witchetty grubs,' Tanya said drily. 'He does have a house on his property, you know. And it's not just *me* going. There'll be other guests there as well. And what's so lucky about being stuck out in the bush for a whole weekend? I'm a city girl—you know that. I hate the bush.'

'But if your friend Simon Devlin is going to be there...'

'He's *not* my friend. He's a legal colleague. And I don't like him one bit. In fact, he's quite insufferable most of the time.'

Ellie raised an eyebrow. 'Could have fooled me. You've barely talked about anybody else since you started working on this case with him. If you dislike him so much, why didn't you send your brief to another barrister?'

'Because my client specifically asked for Simon Devlin, that's why,' Tanya retorted. She added musingly, 'I have a feeling Daddy doesn't like him all that much either. He looked decidedly unimpressed when I mentioned I'd sent a brief to Simon Devlin—and that Simon had accepted it.'

Ellie chuckled. 'Daddy afraid you might get involved with the man, is he? Simon Devlin, brilliant barrister or not, isn't exactly the type of guy Mr Justice Barrington would choose for his only daughter.'

'Oh?' said Tanya, and waited resignedly. She was used to Ellie speaking her mind.

'Well...' Ellie's brown eyes danced, 'Simon Devlin does rather thumb his nose at the Establishment, doesn't he? And your father is definitely "Establishment",' she added without rancour. 'Old family name. Big mansion in Toorak. Holiday homes at Portsea and on the Gold Coast. Member of the hallowed Melbourne Club. Oodles of well-heeled, influential friends...'

She ticked off each point with her fingers, while Tanya rolled her eyes and waited for her to finish.

'Very much one of the old-school-tie brigade, your doting daddy,' Ellie summed up. 'None of which appears to mean that much ——' she snapped her fingers '—to Simon Devlin, the boy from the bush who got where he is today purely on his own ability. Everyone says he's brilliant. He has a mind like a rapier. And his voice in court...' She sighed ecstatically. 'It simply mesmerises the jury! And when he turns on his charm, the women jurors positively swoon.'

'Oh, he's a brilliant barrister, I'll concede that.' Tanya ignored Ellie's remarks—her *ravings*, Tanya considered them—about Simon Devlin's mesmerising voice and charm. 'And there's no denying that most of the other barristers seem to respect him...'

'*And* like him,' Ellie said emphatically. 'He might not be one of your dad's old-school-tie brigade, but he still has plenty of friends in our learned profession.'

'And a few enemies as well, I shouldn't wonder,' Tanya said, her violet-blue eyes narrowing. 'You've only seen him performing in court, Ellie—in public. I've seen his *un*charming side. In private, he's anything *but* mesmerising. He's arrogant, overbearing, sarcastic, abrasive...I can't stand him!'

'Whew! He *has* fired you up!' Ellie tilted her curly dark head at Tanya. 'You know, I reckon you're attracted to him despite yourself—and that's why you're reacting to him the way you are. You're trying to hide it.'

'What utter rubbish!'

But Ellie had the bit between her teeth now and wasn't letting go. 'You can't deny that he's an incredibly attractive hunk of man—pure male, in capital letters. And——' she sighed '—I hear he's still a bachelor!'

'Little wonder,' Tanya said scathingly. 'Can you imagine the kind of life a wife of his would have? She'd end up stuck out in the bush with his kids while *he* went merrily on the way he is now, working in town all week and spending his nights tucked up in his cosy little bachelor pad—conveniently on the loose!'

'Oh?' Ellie's eyes were teasing. 'How do you know his bachelor pad is cosy? You've seen it, have you?'

'No, I haven't!' snapped Tanya. 'I've just heard about it. He has quite a reputation for the ladies, our Mr Simon Devlin, in case you haven't heard.' She curled her lip. 'He always has some gorgeous bird on his arm—or stashed away in his bachelor pad...so they say. Can you imagine that changing once he's married? His poor wife would be lucky to see him at weekends.'

'Maybe when he gets married he'll give up his place in the bush and settle down with his family here in town.'

'Never. You should hear the way he talks about his precious bush. "Home", he calls it. He makes no secret of the fact that that's where he most wants to be. Lord knows why he ever chose to be a hot-shot city barrister in the first place. He should have stayed in the bush.'

Before Ellie could comment on that, Tanya added for good measure, 'As for him being an attractive hunk of man, *I* don't find him the least bit attractive. He's too big. Too tall. Too rough-looking. Too...untidy. His hair is always a mess...and in court his wig is often askew. He always looks to me as if he'd be more comfortable wearing an open-neck shirt and an Akubra hat than a wig and gown. And he's too—too——— ' She cast around for the right word to sum him up.

'Too *male*, darling—is that what you mean?' Ellie asked sweetly. 'He makes you feel...uncomfortable. He doesn't bow and scrape and fall all over you like other guys. He threatens your famed self-possession. Am I right? You'd rather have one of those slick, pompous, polished-to-the-eyeballs clones you grew up with, would you?'

'No, I wouldn't! That is——— ' Tanya shook her head impatiently. 'I don't want *any* man just at the moment, thank you very much. Not any *one* man, that is. I don't want to even think about getting serious or settling down—not for ages and ages. Heavens, I've hardly started my career!'

'You're twenty-six years old, the same as me. And you're in your third year as a fully-fledged solicitor, the same as me. We're not exactly fresh out of university, my love. If a hunk like Simon Devlin asked me to marry him tomorrow, I'd be off like a shot.'

Tanya was momentarily diverted. 'Really? You mean you'd give up the law completely to be a full-time wife and mother?'

'Sure. Wouldn't you?'

'Are you crazy? Throw away all these years of hard work and study? Throw away all the experience I've gained since I qualified? Ellie! I can't believe I heard what I just did.'

'You might feel differently when you meet the right man,' said Ellie with a worldly-wise smile. 'You could always come back to the law later, after your kids started school. I might do that myself,' she mused, 'so long as it's only part-time work, and close to home.'

'You'd be lucky to find any work near your home if you married Simon Devlin,' Tanya pointed out tartly. 'I doubt if there's much call for smart city lawyers in the timbered wilds of Victoria.'

Ellie gave a splutter. 'I was only using Simon Devlin as an example, you dope. I've never even spoken to him.'

Tanya eyed her speculatively. 'You haven't anyone else in mind, have you? You're not keeping something from me?'

Ellie laughed, answering with a grimace, 'No, more's the pity. You at least have Simon Devlin interested in *you*.'

'He's *not* interested in me,' Tanya said impatiently. 'And I'm not interested in him. Haven't you been listening to a word I've been saying?'

'Every word.' Ellie smiled urbanely. 'So you're not interested in him, or he in you. And yet he's invited you to go bush with him this weekend, and you've accepted.'

'Would you stop making it all sound so...so *meaningful*? And so *clandestine*? It's nothing of the sort. I'll spell it out. Simon Devlin and I have this trial starting on Monday. Simon wants to have a final conference with me, and the weekend is the only chance we'll have to get together, because he's tied up for the rest of this week. Are you following so far?'

Ellie nodded meekly. 'And the conference has to be out in the bush?' she asked sweetly. 'Not here in town?'

Tanya inhaled deeply. 'You know Simon Devlin won't stay in town at the weekend unless it's absolutely necessary. Anyway, there happens to be a law function down Warragul way on Saturday night, within a short drive, apparently, of his property. He's invited me and some other people from town to stay at his place for the weekend. Simon, by the way, is one of the after-dinner speakers. He expects me to go along to the dinner with them. I gather he thinks I might learn something.'

'Hmm...' Ellie's dark eyes glinted. 'Well, it still sounds like a cosy weekend to me. *Very* cosy! I bet the other guests are simply a convenient smokescreen, to cover his lecherous desires.'

Tanya gasped. 'Ellie, will you drop it? There is nothing between Simon Devlin and me, and never likely to be.'

'Hmmm,' Ellie said again. 'Does the lady protest too much, I wonder?'

In exasperation, Tanya hurled a cushion at her. *'Ellie,'* she said warningly.

'Sorry.' Ellie ducked. 'Are you driving up in your own car or what?'

At the innocent question Tanya, to her annoyance, flushed. 'I'm driving up with Simon on Friday night. He wants us to get together first thing on Saturday morning before the others—— ' She clamped her mouth shut, realising what she had inadvertently given away.

'Ah!' Ellie pounced. 'Before the others arrive, is that what you were going to say? So you *will* be alone with him . . . for one night, at least. Well, the best of Aussie luck,' she said with a wicked grin, and darted from the room as Tanya reached for another cushion.

'Of course we won't be alone—don't be ridiculous!' Tanya yelled after her. But it was a feeble denial. She had no idea if they were going to be alone in the house on Friday night or not, because Simon Devlin had neglected to fill her in on such details. And his invitation had been issued in such a peremptory manner, seconds before he'd rushed off to court, that she hadn't had a chance to ask.

Knowing the type of man he was, the rough-and-ready bush background he came from, he probably hadn't given a thought to such things as the proprieties. And yet if word got around that the two of them had spent a night together, alone in the bush, she could just imagine the whispers, the conjecture...

Oh, lord, who was she fooling? She gave a splutter of self-mocking laughter as she headed for her bedroom to change into something more comfortable than the tailored suit she'd been wearing all day. Who was going to give a damn if she and Simon Devlin spent a night alone at his place in the bush? None of her sophisticated circle of friends would care, for starters. Most of them had been sleeping around for years. There wasn't one among them who would believe that she, at the ripe old age of twenty-six, had never yet felt sufficiently committed to any man, or attracted enough, to want to give up that most intimate part of her being.

Not even stunningly handsome, highly eligible man-around-town Nick Manning-Smith, whom she had dated for a few months and had been quite smitten with in the beginning, had been able to break down her defences. Unfortunately, Nick had revealed an irritatingly possessive streak which had rapidly cooled her ardour. She hadn't felt ready to be 'possessed'... in any sense of the word. Her feelings for Nick simply hadn't gone deep enough—and, she had realised in the end, they were never likely to. And she had no intention of giving herself to any man without love, without commitment.

She knew that made her a rarity among her swinging crowd, and hopelessly old-fashioned—by their standards, at any rate—but that was too bad. It was just the way she was.

And so she had refused to give in to Nick. And when Nick hadn't accepted that, she had broken off with him—upon which he had accused her of being a tease, a heart-breaker, and a cold-hearted bitch. Stung, Tanya had laughed in his face, hiding her hurt from him, as she had long since learned to cover her inner sensitivity, and her inexperience, with a cool, career-girl sophistication that few people had succeeded in seeing through.

No... her lip quirked. None of her crowd would so much as blink if she spent a night alone with Simon Devlin. Her parents might, if they knew about it, but they were out of town this week. The only one who was likely to care if she stayed overnight with Simon Devlin was herself. And damn it, if she couldn't look after herself by now, her name wasn't Tanya Barrington!

The inexorable ticking of her bedside clock was starting to get on her nerves. It was a relentless reminder that the night was fast slipping away, that she had a witness to interview in the morning, and that she was going to look and feel like death if she didn't get some sleep. If only her mind would stop whirling round in circles! She had managed to dismiss Simon Devlin from her conversation earlier with Ellie, but he wasn't so easy to dismiss from her thoughts. And that annoyed her, because Tanya Barrington had never lost sleep over any man. Not even over Nick Manning-Smith, back in the days when, for a brief time, she had considered him a real heart-throb.

So why lose any sleep over Simon Devlin, a man she didn't even like? A man, furthermore, who seemed to delight in aggravating her every time their paths crossed. Was it *because* he was so aggravating that she was letting him get to her like this? She wasn't used to men treating her the way Simon Devlin did, *speaking* to her the way he did, throwing his weight around in that hatefully arrogant, autocratic, supercilious way of his.

Though *why* she was letting it bother her so much mystified her. It wasn't as if she was the least bit attracted to him, or even cared particularly what he thought of her. He wasn't her type at all—her father would be dead right if his thoughts ran along those lines. She and Simon Devlin had nothing—zilch—in common, other than their involvement in the legal profession. They were complete opposites. They had been brought up in totally different worlds, he in his remote backwoods world—a rough, tough rural world that Tanya knew nothing about and had no wish to know anything about, a world that turned out big raw macho men with brilliant enough minds but the instincts of cavemen...

Her lip twitched faintly. Maybe it was going a bit far to call Simon Devlin a caveman, but that was more or less the image he presented—of a rugged, rough-diamond character who didn't bother to conform and who didn't give a damn what anybody thought of him—a man from an alien world as far as she was concerned, a world with a fascination that entirely escaped her.

While she...she was a city girl through and through— a Barrington, raised in a world of privilege and comfort, a lover of theatres and exclusive shops and fine dining, with tennis and dancing and beach parties thrown in at weekends—a girl who had always felt perfectly at ease in the élite world of Melbourne's high society.

A world Simon Devlin despised, by all accounts. As a highly respected barrister, he could have broken the barriers and entered that exclusive world by now if he had really wanted to, but he'd never bothered to make the effort. Simon shunned the city's social scene, thumbed his nose at glittering opening nights and fashionable restaurants, preferring to take his women to more intimate, less pretentious places. In fact, he avoided city life altogether whenever he could, escaping to his bush retreat at weekends, and discouraging any intrusion into his private life.

Tanya strongly suspected that Simon Devlin had a chip on his shoulder. His abrasiveness towards *her* on the few occasions they had met so far, the way he was known to ride roughshod over people he didn't have any time for, his avoidance of the high life that so many of his peers embraced with enthusiasm, suggested that he still harboured some secret resentment that the doors which were now open to him had been shut in his face for so long.

She was aware, as most people were, that Simon Devlin, son of a timber cutter, had had to claw his way up in the world, putting himself through law school by taking any jobs that were offered, and reaching his present prominence on ability and grit alone, without benefit of family background, influential contacts, or financial support.

She mulled over Simon's barely concealed hostility towards her. He had shown quite plainly that he resented her, that he resented everything she was and everything she stood for.

Yes, he had a chip on his shoulder all right, and he was taking it out on anyone who had had an easier ride.

Tanya felt herself shivering a little as she recalled his expression the first time they had come face to face in his chambers. She remembered the way his eyes had travelled so coldly over her, dwelling for an uncomfortably long moment on her face, until she had been forced to drop her own gaze under his ice-cold scrutiny. His startling coal-grey eyes had held an unfriendly intensity that had shaken her. He had looked almost as if he hated her.

It's my class, the social circles I move in that he hates, not me, she rallied, plumping up her pillow in exasperation and with each savage punch, imagining it was Simon Devlin's autocratic face she was punching.

She recalled his curt opening words, confirming her suspicions.

'Well, so you're Barrington's daughter.'

Just as there was no warmth in his gaze, neither was there any softness in his tone. She had heard the rich timbre of his courtroom voice on one or two occasions in the past, but there was no sign of it on this occasion. It was pitched low, a cold, indifferent drawl, masking whatever emotions he was feeling. Was his chilly aloofness an attempt to cut her down to size, to show her he wasn't impressed by her name, her social position?

'You know my father?' she had responded coolly, meeting his steely gaze with equal steadiness, a tiny flame burning in her eyes, turning the deep blue to glittering violet. She had no intention of being intimidated by this bear of a man, if that was his intention. At the same time, she found herself wishing he weren't so damned tall, so physically overpowering. It meant she had to tilt her head back to look him in the eye, and no doubt that gave him a certain satisfaction, the feeling that he had her at a disadvantage. Well, think again, my learned colleague.

'Our paths have crossed—naturally.'

He was saying that he and her father weren't friends...would never be friends. Which hardly came as a surprise to Tanya. She couldn't see Simon Devlin having any time for a member of the despised Establishment, even an illustrious High Court judge like her father. And she certainly couldn't see her father making any overtures of friendship to Simon Devlin. Anyone without the right connections, who didn't conform to an acceptable pattern and lifestyle—acceptable to her father, that was—would be suspect in Hugh Barrington's eyes. Mr Justice Barrington could be a rather stuffy old snob at times, Tanya mused. But, for all his prejudices and set ways, he was a fine man and a fine judge, and she loved him dearly.

Simon Devlin, rather surprisingly, had, she recalled, broken eye contact first, his eyes flickering downwards, to rove over her soft lips and creamy throat in a way that, infuriatingly, brought a flush to her cheeks. She, Tanya Barrington, blushing under a man's gaze! It wasn't as if she wasn't used to being stared at, to hearing remarks along the lines of, 'You're a *lawyer*? Good lord, I thought you must be a model...or a TV star!' or the classic one she'd heard so many times: 'The girl who has everything...brains *and* good looks!' and half the time you could tell they were also thinking, 'and money too'. She had become a bit jaded by it all...it was so predictable.

And now here was Simon Devlin boldly running his eyes over her, the same as every man she'd ever met. Only she knew, with a twinge of unease, that this time it wasn't the same at all, because this time there was no

flicker of admiration, no softness, no flattery in that
steady gaze, just a cold, assessing appraisal.

Your resentment is showing, Simon Devlin...

'My client should be arriving any minute,' she in-
formed him in cool, clipped tones as she tried to regain
her composure. She didn't lose it often. 'Is there anything you'd care to discuss, Mr Devlin, before he comes?'

He didn't answer straight away. In the pause before
he did, he brought his gaze back to her face and let it
dwell there for what seemed an uncomfortably long
moment. Did he resent her taking the initiative? A mere
solicitor!

'Simon. Please,' he invited languorously. The request
was a formality, not a compliment. It wasn't unusual
for counsel and briefing solicitor to be on first-name
terms in private. 'I'm sure you don't want me calling
you Miss Barrington every time we meet,' he drawled.
'Or should I say *Ms* Barrington?'

'Tanya will be fine.' Something in his tone made her
glance sharply up at him. She caught a glint of derision
in his eyes. Never one to hold back, she demanded
scathingly, 'Do you have something against women solicitors, Mr Devlin?' laying subtle stress on the 'Mr'. She
would call him 'Simon' in her own good time!

He looked down at her from his great height, and again
there was a distinct chill in his eye. 'Far from it,' he
denied, a sardonic eyebrow slanting upwards. 'I only
disapprove of rabidly feminist women solicitors, especially the ones who carry their strident views into their
personal lives, inflicting them on everyone around them.
But with your upbringing, I'm quite sure you can't be
one of those.'

'Ah! So it's my upbringing you disapprove of.'

'Did I say I disapprove of you?'

Tanya shrugged in exasperation, and let it go, thinking, No, you don't have to say it—it's in every fibre of your body. You disapprove of *who* I am, and you disapprove of *what* I am.

Her eyes must have told him more than she intended, because she saw a glimpse of something else in his eye—cynical amusement. He found her reaction amusing, damn him!

'The chip on your shoulder is showing, Simon Devlin,' she accused, her irritation boiling over, drawing the rash retort from her.

Something kindled in the frosty grey depths as Simon answered in a soft, steely voice, so different from the rich, ringing tones he used in court. 'An unwise accusation for a girl who's had an easy rise up the legal ladder on her daddy's coat-tails.'

Tanya gasped, her eyes blazing indigo sparks at him. The insolence of the man! 'That's not true!'

'Isn't it? We'll see.'

Inwardly fuming, she gulped down her anger. He was deliberately baiting her, deliberately trying to make her lose her cool, no doubt believing that that was the way to retain the upper hand. Well, he wasn't going to succeed—on either count! Resolutely, she pulled a mask over her features, the cool mask she'd used so many times before to hide her true feelings, her deep-down vulnerability.

Simon slipped into the chair behind his desk and started shuffling the papers in front of him, his dark head bent and an unruly lock of hair tumbling across his brow. Far from giving him an endearingly boyish air, it made him look, if anything, tougher, rougher, more masculine, and Tanya didn't wonder that some people referred to him as the rough-diamond macho man from the bush.

He looked up abruptly, catching her eye, startling her. She hoped he couldn't read her thoughts! Thrusting a finger at the page in front of him, he barked, 'I want you to chase up these two witnesses and have full proofs of evidence by next week.' His grey eyes lanced her deep blue ones, and she felt tiny, tingling shockwaves shoot through her. For a brief, jolting second she was acutely aware of every tiny fleck, every minute pattern, every pinprick of light in the piercing grey.

It was only with the greatest self-control that she managed not to waver under his gaze. She couldn't understand why he was having this intense effect on her, and it annoyed her that he should be. A man she thoroughly disliked!

Not trusting herself to answer without snapping back—or worse, what if her voice should crack?—Tanya remained silent, merely giving a cool nod, maintaining her impassive mask only with a supreme effort.

'It's a well-prepared brief,' Simon acknowledged, with no softening of his tone. 'All your own work, is it?'

Tanya was speechless—which only seemed to confirm his suspicion, judging by the tightening of his lips. Anger flared inside her, but she was determined not to give him the satisfaction of seeing it, or of seeing her leap to her own defence. Let him think what he damned well pleased! It was no skin off her nose what Simon Devlin thought of her. Plenty of others in the legal profession, who knew her better, thought differently—and would say so if he ever voiced his opinion of her outside these chambers.

It had come as a vast relief when their client, a diffident middle-aged businessman who had been charged with embezzling money, had tapped on the door.

Tanya's thoughts roved back to her second meeting with Simon Devlin, only two days later. They had met, quite by accident, as she was leaving the Supreme Court building after lodging a bail application on behalf of another client. Simon, in wig and gown, was standing at the foot of the steps with a group of barristers, but he broke away when he saw her, tugging the wig from his head as he strode towards her.

'Good morning,' he said, and, though the tilt of his lips could hardly have been called a smile, his greeting was pleasant enough. She paused, squinting up at him, her heart for some reason playing a riotous rhythm all of its own. There was no denying it—he *was* an imposing figure, even more so today with his voluminous black gown swirling round his long legs and his flyaway hair, burnished by the sun, lifting and falling in the breeze.

'Good morning,' she echoed politely, wondering idly what a real smile would do to the strong, rugged planes of his face, and to those hard grey eyes.

'Have you had lunch?' he asked without preamble, and when she shook her head he barked, 'Wait here. Don't move.'

Her jaw dropped as he turned on his heel and headed for the court steps, vanishing a second later through the open doors of the Supreme Court building.

'What the—— ' She clenched her lips. If he thought she was going to wait here for him . . . just like that! She glared at the doors he had disappeared through, and she could still see his image imprinted in the open doorway as clearly as if he were still there. Only now the black gown was the cloak of Dracula, and the horns of Satan protruded from his impossibly untidy head of hair!

She was still standing there, inwardly fuming, when he emerged a few minutes later, minus his Dracula-like gown—wearing, this time, a white shirt and tie.

Without giving her a chance to speak, he caught her arm and propelled her away with a muttered, 'I hope you like seafood.'

She was about to retort that men normally asked her if she was available before imperiously assuming she was going to fall in with their plans, but it seemed petty to protest when she *was* available and she *was* hungry, and they *were* working together on a case, for the duration of which it would be wise to maintain at least a veneer of amicability.

He steered her into a popular seafood restaurant near the law courts, where they were ushered to a quiet corner table.

'I only have half an hour before I have to be back in court,' said Simon, snapping his fingers for service— which was instantly forthcoming. He ordered white wine and fish of the day without even bothering to enquire if that would suit her. Again, to her own surprise, Tanya let it pass. She might as well go along with him while she had no objection to his proposals—it was obvious he was in a hurry—but heaven help Mr Simon Devlin if he suggested anything she wasn't prepared to go along with. She'd come up against masterful men before, and in most cases they had been the ones to come off second best!

'I want to get together once more before the trial starts,' Simon said without preamble. 'But I'll be tied up in court for the rest of this week, and my evenings are committed. We'll have to meet at the weekend.'

She glanced at him in surprise. 'You'll be in town at the weekend?' Didn't he go bush every weekend?

'We won't be meeting here in town. There's a law function in Warragul on Saturday night, not far from my property down that way, and I have some house guests arriving around lunchtime on Saturday. You and I will confer together on Saturday morning before they arrive.'

Tanya's brain was spinning. 'You mean—you want to have a conference up *there*? In the bush?' She heard the dismay in her voice, and knew that he must be able to hear it as well. Well, too bad. He wasn't considering her at all. How many hours would it take her to drive all the way up there and back? She'd been planning to play tennis on Saturday afternoon—and there was a party on Saturday night.

'You have no objection, I trust?' His grey eyes were cold, challenging her to voice one. 'I'll drive you up on Friday night—we'll leave straight after work.'

Friday night? She swallowed—hard. But that would mean staying overnight at his place in the bush...presumably alone with him! The others, he'd said, wouldn't be arriving until Saturday.

He swept on, not giving her a chance to protest. 'You can come to the function in Warragul with us on Saturday night. I'm one of the after-dinner speakers. You may find the evening beneficial.' His eyes, under his flickering eyelids, glittered with the sheen of old pewter. She wondered what was behind that icy glitter. Triumph? Mockery? He must be well aware that she didn't want to come!

'I'll drive you back on Sunday evening when I'm ready to come back,' he added, his tone sardonic.

Would he now? Tanya inhaled deeply. If he expected her to stay for the whole weekend, he was way off beam!

'I'm sorry, but I—I have other commitments on Sunday...'

At once the familiar chill was back in his eyes. 'Oh?' His tone was scathing. 'What? A frolic in the Portsea surf? A high-society barbecue? Something you couldn't possibly miss, of course.'

The very fact that he had hit close to the mark brought a quick, defensive reaction. 'A commitment is a commitment.'

'Well, this time you'll have to break it,' he said, unmoved. 'I'm sorry if you consider your social life more important than your job. I suggest you get your priorities right!'

Her eyes blazed, but what could she say? She could hardly tell him that her reluctance to spend the weekend at his bush property was more to do with *him*—with not wanting to spend any more time with him than was absolutely necessary—than dismay at missing out on her social life. She had never allowed her social activities to interfere with her work.

'Be ready Friday around six o'clock,' he rapped out. 'Bring your weekend bag into the office—there won't be time for you to go home. We'll grab a bite to eat on our way.'

She thrust out her jaw, resenting his cavalier assumption that she would meekly fall in with his plans, resenting his total disregard for her feelings and what she might want. She wasn't going to go down without a fight—not this time!

'I'll drive myself up on Saturday morning,' she said firmly. That way she would avoid having to stay alone with him overnight on Friday, and she would be able to drive home when she liked.

'No, you won't. I want you there bright and early Saturday morning, and I want to make sure you *are* there. You'd never find the place on your own. You'd get lost, arrive late, and put out my whole schedule. I told you, I'm expecting guests for lunch, and I want to have our conference over by the time they arrive. You'll drive up with me the night before.'

Mutiny blazed in her eyes, and she only just caught back the sharp retort that sprang to her lips. Who did this man think he was, ordering her around this way? Did he treat all women solicitors the same way? Or only the ones he considered to be spoiled little rich daddy's darlings—ones who'd had an easy ride up the ladder on their daddies' coat-tails!

She had never felt so angry, or so helpless, in her life.

Even now, as she lay tossing in her bed, the anger was still there... And she had to spend a whole weekend with that intolerable, tyrannical, insufferable man, in *his* unfamiliar world—a rough, remote, unappealing, sure-to-be-dead-boring bush world that she knew nothing about and had no wish to know anything about.

What a hell of a way to spend a perfectly good weekend!

On the drive eastwards from the city in Simon Devlin's comfortable grey Volvo, neither spoke much. The peak-hour traffic demanded Simon's full attention, and when eventually they reached the city outskirts and the traffic began to thin out Simon pushed a button on the panel in front of him and the rousing strains of a Mahler symphony filled the interior of the car.

'You don't mind?' he asked, but the question was merely rhetorical. He was already settling back into his seat, making himself comfortable, having already set the car to cruise control. He wasn't even looking at her, still less expecting her to say no.

'Go right ahead...I love Mahler,' Tanya replied, letting her head loll back against the seat, hiding her irritation behind a serene smile. He did turn his head as the composer's name rolled off her lips, but she pretended not to notice, allowing her eyelids to flutter and close. She was determined not to give him the satisfaction of seeing her lose her cool. That, she had decided, should be the best way to deal with Mr Simon Devlin.

They listened to the music in an almost companionable silence until, some time later, she felt the car swing round and come to a halt.

'Are we here already?' she asked, blinking. Dusk was falling outside, and she saw, with a sinking heart, that they had pulled up outside an old two-storey sandstone pub.

'Any objection to a counter tea?' asked Simon, throwing open his door and unwinding his long frame. 'You'll always find a good steak here at the Arms.'

He was out of the car before she had time to answer, as usual not even waiting for a nod from her. Tanya threw open her own door and stepped out before he could come round and open it for her. Not that he looked as if he had any intention of doing any such thing!

I'll bet he only acts the gentleman with those fluffy-headed floozies he squires around town, she growled under her breath. To Simon Devlin, it was plain that she was just an irritatingly necessary legal colleague—someone he had to put up with and who didn't need any special consideration.

The pub was noisy and crowded with locals, un-savoury-looking characters, Tanya thought in distaste, eyeing them warily as they crowded round the bar, swilling their beer in a haze of cigarette smoke, their gravelly, good-humoured chatter punctuated by loud gusts of ribald laughter.

'I realise it's not the Regent,' Simon murmured drily, noting Tanya's set expression. 'But make no mistake, these guys are good honest workers—truckies, foresters, road-workers—who get up a healthy thirst after a long hard day's work.' He looked down at her with a look that seemed to imply that she wouldn't know what a long hard day's work *was*.

'Relax, Tanya.' His lip curled faintly. 'We won't be staying in here. After we've got ourselves a drink and placed our order for dinner, we'll move into the dining-room next door. What'll you have? A beer? Brandy-and-dry? I suggest nothing too fancy.'

Tanya glowered at him. Was he afraid she'd order an exotic cocktail or a glass of French champagne? Nor-mally she drank very little, usually settling for a mineral water or a glass of wine with dinner, but she felt she needed something stronger at this moment, if only to fortify herself against Simon Devlin.

'A Scotch'll do, thanks. On the rocks.'

He nodded curtly, his eyes flicking coldly away. He's not surprised, she thought with a curious, perverse sat-isfaction, to hear Mr Justice Barrington's pampered little darling ordering the hard stuff. Well, if he thinks that's me, let him keep his misconceptions. If he goes on de-spising me, and I go on despising him, we won't be in any danger of getting too close, too friendly. Simon Devlin was not a man she would want to get close to— ever. They were light years apart—in their thinking, in their lifestyles, in their backgrounds, in everything. What other man would dare to bring her to a place like this? Had he chosen this awful old pub deliberately? Had he calculatedly thrust those 'good, honest workers' under her nose to make her feel more alien, more out of her depth, more miserably at odds with his rough-and-tumble bush world than she already was?

She felt a bit better after the Scotch. The dining-room, which had struck her as starkly depressing when she first walked in, with its chrome tables and chairs and its bare linoleum floor and the jabbering TV set perched on the wall, now seemed sensibly functional, even moderately inviting. The bunches of white daisies on each table were real, not plastic, and the generous array of salads and fresh bread rolls on the sideboard was beginning to make her mouth water. And at least the place looked scrupulously clean.

When the Bill Cosby Show came on the television, she even found herself chuckling aloud at one point—surprisingly, along with Simon, though when she glanced round at him his expression was already settling back into its former languor, as if he had quickly regretted that moment of shared intimacy.

It was then that their steaks arrived—the biggest T-bones Tanya had seen in her life.

'I'll never be able to eat all this!' she protested, laughing.

'Try,' Simon urged. 'Otherwise you'll be mighty hungry by breakfast-time tomorrow.'

She gulped nervously. She didn't want to think about breakfast, because that meant thinking about the night ahead—alone with Simon Devlin. Had she been mad to accept his offer of a lift this evening? But he'd given her no choice! Not that it was her company he'd wanted—

he'd just wanted to make sure she was there at his bidding first thing in the morning for their conference.

'It's delicious!' she heard herself gushing a moment later in surprise. 'It's so tender.'

'Good,' he said, his tone as impassive as his expression. If the beer had mellowed him, Tanya reflected acidly, he wasn't letting it show!

Twenty minutes later they were on their way again, leaving the small town behind—a town much like any other small Australian country town she had ever driven through, Tanya thought, unimpressed, with its corner pub, its group of uninspiring shops, its general look of untidiness—and hardly a living soul in sight. No late-night shopping out here, obviously. And who'd want to shop here anyway?

As the Volvo picked up speed, Simon remarked casually, 'We're about halfway,' and she groaned inwardly. Only halfway, and it could only get worse, the further into the hills they went!

Were they to see nothing but boring gum-trees and an endless expanse of dry grass and scrubby bushes from now on? The uninviting terrain made her heart shrink. What did Simon Devlin see in this dreary, depressing landscape? Why ever had she agreed to come?

She turned her head to murmur tartly, 'Only halfway, you said...'

'Mm,' he said absently. He was squinting through the windscreen. 'Looks like rain clouds ahead. Let's hope so.'

She gaped at him. 'You hope we run into rain?' Surely rain was the last thing they needed. Wet roads, slush, and an even more dismal outlook! Not that they'd be able to see anything before long—it was growing darker by the minute.

'We've had no rain for a couple of weeks,' Simon explained. 'God knows we need it. You can see how dry everything is.'

'Couldn't be much drier,' she agreed.

Something in her tone brought his head round sharply. Their eyes met before she could mask the disillusionment she knew must be there. Though he made no comment, she saw his expression harden, and knew he was displeased. Simon Devlin wouldn't appreciate criticism of his beloved bush world . . . least of all by a spoiled rich girl fresh from the big city.

They ran into rain about ten minutes later, huge pinging drops to begin with, spattering the windscreen like noisy pellets from an air-gun, followed by steady, driving rain that kept the windscreen wipers working overtime for the rest of the trip. It was difficult to see the road ahead, and each time another car came towards them Tanya tensed as the headlights blazed into the wet windscreen, momentarily blinding her—and no doubt having the same effect on Simon, though he made no comment.

He appeared to be finding the drive no strain at all. The appalling conditions didn't seem to be affecting him in the least. 'Let's hope it's raining at home,' he shouted over the din, and she thought glumly, Oh, great. A wet weekend in the bush. That's all I need!

'Is it a sealed road all the way?' she asked, with a depressing picture in her mind of a bogged Volvo and a long walk through the mud in her new Gucci shoes.

'All but the last few kilometres,' said Simon, and she would have sworn there was a malevolent grin playing about his lips. He's enjoying this, damn him, she realised in disbelief. The more miserable this weekend becomes, the better he'll like it. The man's a sadist!

'Don't worry,' he consoled, 'we won't get bogged, if that's what you're afraid of. It's an all-weather road.'

As long as he keeps *on* the road, Tanya reflected anxiously, imagining the soft earth on either side rapidly turning into a mud trap.

Through the curtain of rain she could dimly see that they were driving through a forest of some kind, the trees breathtakingly tall, with incredibly long straight trunks which thrust upward to disappear into the misty cloud. At the foot of the trees a tangle of bracken and lacy ferns quivered under the onslaught of the rain.

At the same time, the terrain was growing more undulating. The road wound round and round and swooped up and down until Tanya began to feel decidedly queasy. She shrank lower in her seat, mute and miserable, and yet still defiant, determined not to give in to the nausea that was threatening to sweep over her.

The rain was still tumbling down when Simon finally swung the car off the bitumen road on to the unsealed section he had warned about earlier. Even though he had assured her it was an all-weather road, Tanya, arousing herself with a tiny shake, was relieved to see that it wasn't under water, or already a quagmire, and was doubly comforted by the sound of solid crunching stones and gravel under the wheels.

After what seemed an eternity, after more tortuous bends and rises, with only the ribbon of road ahead and a border of dismal trees visible in the beam of the car's headlights, Simon turned off the road to pass through an open gateway into what Tanya assumed was a driveway, though she very soon began to have her doubts. It was little more than a bush track—the gravel surface at least making it passable—winding aimlessly, or so it seemed, through the soggy bush. Nobody's driveway could go on and on like this, could it? she wondered in growing despair.

CHAPTER TWO

'THERE'S the house, straight up ahead.' There was something different in Simon's tone now, a stirring of excitement, a low rumble of pride.

Tanya saw lights ahead, just visible through the blurred windscreen. Somebody must have turned them on. Did Simon have a live-in housekeeper? She felt a surge of relief. Or maybe he had a wife tucked away out here after all...a wife he'd told nobody about. Or a live-in lover?

She thought of the succession of women Simon Devlin squired around town, and compressed her lips. A man who chased women in the city was just as likely to chase them in the bush. And what a convenient place to hide them! For all she knew, Simon Devlin could lead a positively debauched existence out here in the bush. How did she know he wasn't a sort of hippie Bluebeard, with a string of earthy females at his fingertips to help while away his weekends in the bush—as a change, no doubt, from the more sophisticated beauties he squired around town during the week!

A nervous giggle rose to her throat. And what category do you think you come into, Tanya Barrington? Earthy— or sophisticated? Or are you a brand new category altogether? Was Bluebeard now trying to lure his female *legal* colleagues into his bacchanalian clutches?

She cast a furtive glance at Simon's strong, rigid profile, which in the dimness seemed to have taken on a menacing, almost demonic aura. She sat up sharply.

For Pete's sake, Tanya, snap out of it! Have those wretched bends softened your brain? You're not going to be alone out here in the bush with Simon Devlin. There is obviously someone else in the house, and there will be others arriving tomorrow. You'll be quite safe!

Oh, lord, listen to her! As if there was any danger! Simon Devlin, barrister-at-law, wasn't the least bit interested in her as a *woman*, as a sex object. She was simply a solicitor who was briefing him, and it suited him to have a legal conference with her here instead of in town, no matter how inconvenient it might be to her.

The darkness and the swirling rain almost completely hid the house's immediate environs, except for a shadowy wall of trees and a few dripping branches that overhung the driveway. The house itself was a surprise. Tanya had been half expecting to see an old iron-roofed farmhouse, possibly with sagging verandas and rickety front steps, but instead the house looked surprisingly modern, all angles and soaring lines and huge floor-to-ceiling windows ablaze with lights.

Simon pressed a remote control device which automatically opened the doors of the double garage underneath the house. He drove straight in, observing drily, 'Now you won't have to get your feet wet.'

'Thoughtful of you,' she murmured as she opened her door and stepped out, again not waiting for him to do the honours. Simon was already out, heading for the boot at the rear of the car, where he had stacked her weekend bag and his own briefcase. As she reached for her bag, he handed her his briefcase instead.

'I'll carry your bag.' As he hauled it out, he muttered, 'What have you got in here—your entire wardrobe?'

Her chin rose. 'I wasn't sure what I'd need, or what the weather was going to be like up here in the hills, so

I stuffed in a bit extra.' Just as well too, she thought huffily, if it's going to be wet and cold and miserable. It's supposed to be early autumn, not winter! She was thankful she *had* thrown in an extra sweater or two and her favourite knee-high leather boots. Not that the rain had brought a drop in the temperature so far, she noticed—it was even warmer and muggier, if anything.

'We tend to be pretty informal out here in the bush,' drawled Simon. 'I hope you haven't brought your full range of designer gear with you.'

Tanya flushed. She'd brought a bit of everything—just in case.

'Well, you did say you were having other guests,' she said defensively. 'I'm sure you'll want me to look presentable when they come. And for the dinner tomorrow night.'

'It's just a dinner, not a society ball,' Simon pointed out, sarcasm lacing his words. 'I'd give the family diamonds and the ballgown a miss, if I were you. I, on the other hand, promise not to wear my frayed jeans and gumboots.'

'How considerate of you!' Glowering, she followed him through a doorway and up a carpeted flight of stairs. She wouldn't be surprised if he had invited her here simply to humiliate her in front of his other guests, with the intention of bringing her down a peg or two. Well, good luck to him!

At the top of the stairs they passed through a spacious games-room with a billiard table, a wall unit displaying a television set and some impressive stereo equipment, and soft armchairs arranged around a huge open fireplace which looked as if it would provide welcome warmth on chilly winter evenings. The walls were of timber and an unusual rough-textured brick, and the

ceiling was cathedral style, with heavy dark beams
slanting upwards to a point way, way up. Again, not
quite what she had been expecting of Simon Devlin's
bush retreat!

There was a glint of mockery in his eyes as he turned
his head and caught her expression, but he said only,
'I'll show you to your room first. Then we'll have some
coffee. Follow me.'

'Fine,' she said, trailing obediently behind. Coffee
sounded great. 'You have room here to put up several
guests for the weekend?' she asked curiously—and at
once could have bitten off her tongue, realising how the
question must sound to a man with a chip on his shoulder
about his disadvantaged upbringing. Would he see it as
condescending? She hadn't meant it to be.

But the merest flickering of his eyelids was his only
reaction. 'Adequate room,' he said, his tone droll now,
concealing his private thoughts. 'There are four bedrooms—mine, incidentally, is the one at the far end.'

Tanya flushed. Now why was he bothering to tell her
that? she wondered, instantly suspicious. As if she cared
where his bedroom was. She certainly wouldn't be
seeking it out!

She saw the taunting light in his eye, and her flush
deepened. He was just teasing her, trying to make her
lose her cool for his own cynical amusement.

She tossed her head, and threw him a scathing look,
not bothering to grace his remark with one of her own.
So, she thought. *Four* bedrooms. Did he often have
guests for the weekend, then? Or was it his intention one
day to fill all those bedrooms with his own children?
Having plenty of kids would keep his wife happy and
busy at home while he was working all week in town...

'It's all right.' Again that taunting tilt of his brow. 'You won't have to share a room with anyone, if that's what you're afraid of.'

She took a quick, sharp breath at his perceptiveness. She *had* braced herself for the possibility...not dreaming she was coming to a modern house with four bedrooms and enough space to fit a small army! The prospect of having to bunk down with a stranger, even if only for one night, had been just one other thing about this weekend that had been filling her with dread.

'I wonder if I know any of the other guests,' she said as they passed through his spacious kitchen. If it was a law function that was bringing them here, she just might have met some of them.

'You might have come across Joe Camillieri in the course of your work. He's the director of Sanctuary House, the drug rehabilitation centre.'

She nodded. 'Yes, I have met him.' She'd been there a few times to see clients who had been charged with drug-related offences.

'He's bringing one of his staff—a girl called Amanda Scott. I believe they've just become engaged. They're the only two who'll be staying here overnight—aside from us. There'll be one extra dropping in for lunch tomorrow.'

'Oh.' Tanya gulped. So there were only two others staying the night! A cosy couple. Well, if Simon Devlin had any thought of pairing off with *her*...

For a second their eyes clashed. Hers were chilly, his mocking.

'Our extra lunch guest tomorrow is the local magistrate, Dimity Donohue, who also happens to be a neighbour of mine. She's responsible for the function tomorrow night, as a matter of fact. She's organising it.'

Tanya's eyes narrowed. Dimity Donohue, local magistrate, neighbour and ... a woman! Was Simon involved with her? she wondered idly. Even if he wasn't, she could breathe more easily now. She was unlikely to find herself paired off with Simon while another woman was present!

Nobody came to meet them—and Simon didn't call out to summon anybody. Where was the person who had switched on all the lights? Or had they come on automatically? Simon, being away so often, could, she supposed, have them on a time switch, to deter would-be burglars. Only surely he wouldn't have to worry about burglars way out here!

Wherever *here* was. Because of the murky darkness and the blinding rain on their way here, she had no idea how isolated the place was, or how far it was from the adjoining property, or the nearest town, if there *was* a town nearby.

She shivered—more a shudder than a shiver. Here she was, buried in some remote part of the Victorian highlands, miles from the main highway, miles from anywhere civilised, quite alone with a man she barely knew, didn't like, and wasn't even sure she could trust! Fortunately, he didn't appear to be the least bit interested in her in any personal way, in any *lecherous* way... There, had certainly been no suggestive remarks or rakish leers to suggest there could be a wolf lurking under that cool, cynical, contemptuous exterior of Simon Devlin's. His invitation to spend the weekend here in the bush with him—along with *others*, she must remember—had been made in a purely businesslike manner, for a purely businesslike reason—so that they could get together to discuss

Monday's trial. With a law function thrown in, which
she might find 'beneficial'.

Despite herself, her mouth twitched. The thought of
Simon Devlin harbouring wicked designs on Tanya
Barrington—who in his eyes was a spoiled socialite first,
a questionable lawyer second—was so outlandish it was
almost laughable. She didn't appeal to him any more
than he appealed to her!

The bedroom wing was at the far end of the house,
access being along a wide passage hung with Australian
paintings. It struck Tanya afresh that it was a very large
house, for one person. They hadn't even stepped into
the illuminated front rooms yet—which she assumed
would be the formal living area.

The bedroom which Simon led her into was another
surprise. As he switched on the soft amber wall light
inside the doorway, she found herself in a quite charming
room every bit as big as her old bedroom back in her
parents' home in Toorak, and considerably larger than
any of the rooms at the flat she shared with Ellie. Under
the curtained window was a big brass bed covered with
a multi-coloured doona, and there were built-in cup-
boards the full length of one wall. A door in another
wall suggested there could even be an en-suite bathroom.

Yes, it was quite a house, this rural retreat of Mr
Simon Devlin's. No wonder he liked to come here so
often! Pity it was so far from town . . . and worse, stuck
out here in the bush. Now if it had been down along the
coast somewhere . . .

'Nice room,' she commented. 'Are all the bedrooms
like this?'

'Pretty much the same.' He arched an eyebrow. 'I hope
you'll be comfortable.'

There was a glint of silvery laughter in his eyes—derisive laughter. He knew that the room, the house, had surprised her...knew that she had been expecting to have to rough it out here in the bush, that she had been dreading what she would find.

'Unpack whatever you want to unpack and then come to the kitchen,' he said, heading for the door. She frowned after him, tempted to shout, 'Yes, *sir*!' If he would just once make a request instead of turning everything into a command! With a sigh, she turned her attention to her bag. It really wasn't worth getting steamed up about. She ought to be used to barristers who enjoyed throwing their weight around. In Simon Devlin's case, of course, his personal antagonism would hardly be softening his attitude towards her!

The welcome aroma of freshly brewed coffee assailed her nostrils as she made her way to the kitchen a short while later, having slipped out of the businesslike skirt and jacket she had worn to work, exchanging them for comfortable burgundy slacks and a cream silk shirt.

Simon glanced round as she walked in. He too had changed, she noticed. She had only seen him in a suit before, or a wig and gown, but in his thigh-hugging jeans and black T-shirt, both of which revealed muscles and sinews previously only hinted at, and with his unruly dark hair in a more rumpled state than ever, he looked—she gulped, she couldn't help it—even taller, even broader across the shoulders, even more overpowering than before, more—Ellie's word leapt to mind—more *masculine*. She found it distinctly unsettling, even a trifle disturbing. Which irked her no end, to think that the man could affect her this way—in this purely *carnal* fashion. A man she thoroughly disliked!

Suddenly she wished with all her heart that she had insisted on driving herself up here tomorrow morning, even if she'd had to leave town at the crack of dawn to get here! Only knowing her sense of direction, she would have got hopelessly lost, and Simon Devlin would *not* have been amused. Especially if his other guests had arrived before she did, putting paid to his planned private conference with her.

'Black or white?' Simon was asking, and she had to swallow hard before answering, 'Black, thanks,' as she tried to regain her composure. So the man had more than his share of animal magnetism. Well, so what? He'd need more than a powerful set of shoulders and a compelling physical presence to attract her in any real sense of the word—let alone to make her like him. She wasn't a young girl fresh out of school, to be fooled by a purely physical reaction.

'And a piece of freshly baked sultana cake?' Without waiting for an answer, Simon sliced off a piece, buttered it and handed it to her. It smelt very fresh—very enticing. 'My sister's speciality... She thoughtfully left it here for us when she popped over earlier to switch on the lights.'

'Your sister?' How peculiar her voice sounded, wobbly, quite unlike her own. She felt like giving herself a good hard kick. What a sorry pass it was when the sight of a man's muscles started affecting a girl's voice!

'My sister Maggie,' said Simon. To Tanya's relief he turned away to cut a piece of cake for himself as he spoke. 'She lives on the property over the hill with her husband Mike and my two devilish young nephews. I'm lucky having them living so close by—they have to pass by here on their way to the local town and the school, and they tend to keep a watchful eye on the place when I'm not here. Let's go and sit in the lounge.'

How convenient for him, Tanya thought rather waspishly as she fell into step behind him. Having his sister living close by to bake cakes and switch on lights and generally keep a watchful eye on the place for him! It wouldn't surprise her if his sister also did his cleaning and his shopping and even tended his garden for him—presuming they *had* formal gardens out here in the bush! She had no idea if Simon's property was merely a house surrounded by some form of garden, or if it was a farm of some kind—or simply virgin bush. She had never bothered to ask.

Something else struck her. 'Your sister knew I was driving up with you?' Maggie had left the cake 'for us', Simon had said. Not 'for me'.

'Sure, I mentioned we were driving up together. Did you want me to keep you a secret?' His eyes taunted her, and colour rushed to her cheeks.

'Of course not...' Her voice trailed away as the impact of the room they were entering hit her. It was actually two rooms, a huge open-style living-room and a formal dining area, separated by a massive free-standing stone fireplace with a shiny copper flue.

Floor-to-ceiling windows ran the full length of the room, and the glow from the lights within the room illuminated a balcony outside with a jutting timber overhang that prevented the rain from striking the windows—just as it must keep the sun at bay in the hot weather. The walls, as in the games-room, were an artistic combination of brick and timber, hung with tapestries and a selection of Australian paintings—oils and watercolours—with trees and ferns predominating. Beige-coloured leather armchairs were dotted about the room, and there were colourful rugs scattered across the gleaming floorboards.

The focal point of the stunning room was a rich brown baby grand piano. Its ornate legs and ornamental finish suggested it was many years old.

'Do you play?' she asked Simon curiously as she settled into the armchair he had indicated. Had he acquired the piano purely as a status symbol, an investment, a pretty piece of furniture for his guests to look at and admire? she wondered with a touch of mild scorn. This room— the whole place—seemed to cry out, See what I've achieved! Isn't it magnificent? And I did it all on my own!

Or was she doing him an injustice, simply looking for something to criticise? The place was as comfortable, as liveable-in, as it was attractive. Was there anything so wrong in that? He spent a lot of his time here, and by all accounts intended to spend a lot more in the future.

Simon pulled up a coffee-table to set their cups down on, then sat down himself. 'I make a few fumbling attempts to play, when I have the time. I never had any formal lessons. My mother taught me at home.'

'This was her piano?' asked Tanya, involuntarily showing her surprise. She had been under the impression that Simon's parents were simple country folk. Wasn't his father a timber cutter? This looked a very grand piece of furniture for a lowly timber cutter's wife!

She saw a hard gleam leap to Simon's eyes, and felt a prickle of shame. He had noted her surprise, and knew full well what she was thinking. She thought in self-disgust, I'm thinking the way my father would. Which makes me just as big a snob as he!

Simon took a bite of Maggie's sultana cake and swallowed it before he answered. 'My mother inherited the piano from her parents—she was an only child—and she brought it with her when she married my father. He had to knock down a wall to fit it into the house.' Some emotion flicked across his face, and was gone. 'My mother was a beautiful pianist.'

Was? 'Where is your mother now?' she asked tentatively. If Simon had the piano now...

'She and my father live where they've always lived, in the first house they ever built, on the fringes of the local township, a kilometre or so from here. My father retired some years ago—he's in his seventies now. They both potter about quite happily in the old place, with their chooks and their vegetables. My father likes to come over here now and then too, to lend a hand.'

So he had his father dancing attendance on him as well as his sister! Lucky Simon.

'Your parents are content to go on living in their original home while this magnificent place of yours lies empty all week?' Tanya cursed her unruly tongue, but the question intrigued her. Surely there would be more than enough room here for the three of them?

Then again... She narrowed her gaze, weathering Simon's sharp stare without flinching. Maybe it wasn't so surprising, knowing his reputation for the ladies, that he would want his country retreat all to himself... so that he could be private when he came.

'I suppose to someone like you, it must seem incongruous, difficult to understand, that anyone would prefer a ramshackle old farmhouse to a place like this,' Simon drawled, his eyes like flint, his voice hard. 'These trappings—— ' he waved a hand '—don't mean a thing to my parents. They love their house... their few hectares of land. They're comfortable there, and they're near their friends. They feel close to where all their memories are. That's the kind of people they are.' His voice, Tanya noted, was mellowing now as he spoke of his parents, showing a human side to him that she hadn't glimpsed before. 'Neither of them will ever move. Not voluntarily.'

'But doesn't your mother miss her piano?' In for a penny, in for a pound, Tanya thought, her coffee-cup poised halfway to her lips.

'My mother can't play any more, unfortunately. She has arthritis badly in both hands.' The hardness was back in his voice, and Tanya took a quick sip of her coffee to cover the gulp that rose to her throat.

'And my sister Maggie doesn't play—she was never interested. Nor was my older brother Christopher, who's living in Adelaide now with his wife Carol. I suppose you play like an angel,' Simon added with a tinge of sarcasm.

Tanya tilted her fair head at him. 'Why do you say that?'

'Don't all young ladies who pass through exclusive private schools learn how to play the piano?'

'Actually, I learned the violin.'

'Is that so? Do you still play?'

Was he really interested, she wondered sceptically, or just making polite conversation? Impossible to tell from his expression.

'Sometimes,' she said. 'When Ellie's not at home.'

'Who's Ellie?'

'We share a flat. She's a solicitor too. We went to the same school, but to different universities. We've always kept in touch, though. She moved in with me after she graduated.'

Simon brushed aside her mention of Ellie. 'So, you don't live with your parents.' She saw something that might have been surprise flicker far back in his cool grey eyes.

'I'm twenty-six years old,' she said tartly. 'I haven't lived at home for years. I lived in the flat on my own for three years before Ellie joined me.'

'You mean you've been supporting yourself all this time?' Now he looked disbelieving.

A frown clouded her brow. What was this, an inquisition? 'Yes, I've been supporting myself—though I did have some help while I was at university,' she admitted with a tilt of her chin. She wasn't ashamed of it—her parents could afford it, and it had given her a sense of independence living away from home. Her chin lifted a notch higher. 'I dare say you'll be gratified to learn that the flat Ellie and I share actually belongs to my father, so we're obliged to pay only a nominal rent. Satisfied?'

'Just curious,' he said, without apology.

Tanya swung her head away. 'Is it still raining outside?' she asked to change the subject. She could no longer hear the pattering of raindrops on the roof, and through the sweeping expanse of glass she could see nothing but a great black void. It must be a great black *soggy* void by now, she thought in dismay.

'I don't think so.' Simon followed her glance. There was a vaguely disgruntled note in his voice, as if he had been hoping it would go on raining all night. Didn't he care about his weekend guests? 'Ah, well...' He lifted his great shoulders in a gesture of resignation. 'It was good soaking rain while it lasted. Every little bit helps at this time of year.'

'Do you have much property here to look after, Simon?' She was curious, despite her lack of any real interest in his remote, sodden bushland world.

'Three hundred odd hectares. The land on one side
of the house slopes down to a river. To the rear, it's
undulating country, with a backdrop of densely timbered mountains. We have some flat land to the east.
It's similar to the front, which you saw as we drove in.'

She had seen nothing! Only murky, dripping trees and
a swirl of bleak, misty rain.

'Is it just natural bush, Simon?' she asked curiously.
'Or are you into sheep or cows or...' She waved a vague
hand, feeling abysmally ignorant about this part of the
world. 'Or something else?'

'Something else. I grow trees.'

Now she was the one who was surprised. 'Trees?'
Weren't there enough trees around here already? Then
she remembered that Simon had been brought up in the
timber industry, and that this was a forestry area, so
maybe it was only logical that he should have thought
of planting a forest of his own. 'You mean—you're
growing trees commercially?' she ventured, only too
aware that she knew nothing at all about the subject.
She half expected him to snap her head off with a sarcastic, 'Well, I'm not growing them for fun!'

But he didn't snap. 'It will be a commercial prop-
osition...in time. At least, I sincerely hope it will. In
the meantime, I'm having fun working towards that
goal.'

So for now, it *was* just fun. Well, a hard-working city
barrister needed a few leisure-time hobbies, she acknowledged. Simon's hobby was growing trees in the
bush. Her hobbies were tennis and swimming and the
theatre and similar relaxed pursuits with her friends in
the city. Each to his own, she supposed.

'More coffee?' Simon asked. He was looking at her
speculatively, as if trying to work out what thoughts were

running through her head. She had a feeling he wouldn't
appreciate her sharing them with him. He didn't need
to be reminded how different their lifestyles were!

'No, thanks.' She glanced at her watch. 'Time I turned
in,' she said. And as she uttered the words, she was suddenly acutely conscious of being alone in this huge
remote house with Simon, with this man she barely knew,
who kept surprising her, even sparking her interest on
occasion, despite her steadfast reluctance to find anything of interest here in this unfamiliar, out-of-the-way
place. She reached for her empty cup and plate, and
found herself gripping them like a lifeline.

'I could always ask my sister to come over and spend
the night,' Simon offered casually, 'if you're worried
about the proprieties. It would only take a phone call.'

His tone was laconic, indifferent. Plainly, the proprieties didn't bother *him* in the least.

Why then should they bother her? She looked him
straight in the eye. 'That won't be necessary,' she said
evenly. 'I'll just lock my door.'

'*That* won't be necessary either,' he said dampen-
ingly, and she flushed. He was telling her she would be
quite safe from any nocturnal advances from him!

She flicked back her silky mane of fair hair. 'Well, as
long as *we* know the proprieties are being observed, that's
all that matters, isn't it?' She rose as she spoke.

His eyelids flickered as he stood up too. 'You're not
worried about your reputation?' he asked smoothly.
'About setting tongues wagging?'

Tanya shrugged. 'Who's going to know or care if we're
alone here or not? Anyway, people have talked about
me before and I've survived. It's what *I* know to be the
truth that matters.'

He seemed to digest that for a moment. 'Well, as one of the swinging Toorak set, I expect you've set tongues wagging before. I dare say, with your name and background, you can afford to thumb your nose at a bit of tiresome gossip.'

'Mr Devlin,' she said in rising exasperation, 'I realise you have little time for city people, and even less for people with a certain...background. But don't you try putting me into a neat little slot. You'll find I don't fit.'

'I'm glad to hear it.' He was unperturbed. Probably sceptical too, she thought with an inward grimace. 'Want me to see you to your room?' he asked, his tone silky now.

Her blue eyes flared, but she managed to keep her cool. The man was deliberately trying to push her off balance—so that he could retain the upper hand.

'I'm sure I can find my own way, thanks.'

'In that case, you run along.' He took her cup and plate from her. 'I'm going to listen to some Mozart for a while. I bought a new compact disc today.'

She was tempted to ask which particular work it was, but was afraid he might invite her to stay and listen too. And she had no intention of staying around until he was ready to go to bed too. Best to escape now, before an already edgy situation had a chance to turn decidedly awkward.

CHAPTER THREE

TANYA decided to take a shower before going to bed. For some reason she felt hyped-up and wide awake. Standing under a stream of soaking hot water for a while might relax her and help her to sleep.

She undressed without bothering to draw the curtains. Somehow she didn't think peeping Toms would be a problem out here in a house set deep in three hundred odd hectares of private property.

It still wasn't cold, and she didn't bother about a wrap as she stepped into the en-suite bathroom. The shower recess was hidden behind a flimsy floral curtain. As she whipped the curtain aside and prepared to step in, she let out a scream, at the same time recoiling in horror. There was an enormous spider splayed out on the white wall tiles, only inches from the hot water tap. An ugly great thing with a fat brown body and the longest, hairiest legs she had ever seen.

She stood transfixed, trembling from head to toe as if the horrid thing had actually crawled over her naked body. She could still hear her bloodcurdling scream echoing in her ears, and the only other sound she could hear was the pounding of her own heart.

She didn't hear the bedroom door being flung open, was only vaguely aware of advancing footsteps. Simon burst into the bathroom before she had a chance to snatch up a towel.

In the longest split second she had ever known, she was flamingly conscious of his smoky gaze sweeping over her bare body. With a gasp she grabbed the fluffy white towel draped over the rail and bundled it around her nakedness, all too aware that her shoulders and long slim legs were still glaringly visible.

She backed away—from the shower recess, not from Simon. At this precise moment, she was more fearful of the spider than of Simon Devlin. Already her gaze was swinging away from Simon, back to the spider on the wall. If it moved, she knew she would scream again.

'There's a tarantula in the shower!' she gasped. 'A— a huge one!'

He brushed past her without a word, and she would have sworn by the faint curl of his lip that he was laughing at her.

She stood shivering—not from cold, but from shock and reaction—while Simon cupped the great spider in his bare hands and gently released it through the open window.

'But it might c-come back in!' she yelped.

With a shrug, he obligingly pulled the window shut.

'The rain must have driven the poor fellow inside,' he said calmly. 'He wouldn't have hurt you. It was just a Huntsman. They're quite harmless.'

Tanya bit her lip. She felt a bit foolish now. Now that the spider was safely out of the way! She had always had a phobia about spiders—the big hairy variety, at any rate.

'I'm sorry I screamed,' she added in a small voice. 'Stupid of me.' It had been a reflex action—the scream was out before she could stop it. Not that she would have been game enough to dispose of the creature herself. She would still have had to call for Simon. If the wretched thing had jumped at her, or run down her arm, she would have died of fright. She still felt as though it was crawling all over her. She shuddered violently at the gruesome thought.

Simon reached out and grasped her bare shoulders with both hands, his thumb-tip gently kneading her soft flesh. 'You're trembling like a leaf,' he said, sounding surprised. 'You really did get a fright, didn't you?'

'I—I wasn't expecting it to be there. And it was so—so big!' Part of her wished he would let her go, and part of her wished he would keep on with his soothing rubbing, though it was hard to know if it was relaxing her or making her tremble more!

'He was rather a big one,' Simon conceded with a smile. It was a comforting smile, devoid of any discernible mockery, and her trembling began to subside. 'I thought there must have been a snake in the bath at the very least,' he murmured. His smile broadened. It was quite an attractive smile, she noted in surprise, though there was something devilish about it at the same time. 'Actually, I did find a snake in the bath once,' he added.

Her head snapped back. '*Snakes* come into your house as well?' He must be kidding! Snakes in the *bath*?

'Don't worry, it's unlikely it will ever happen again—and certainly not this weekend, after that rain. But yes, I actually did find a snake in the bath once—a black one, about three feet long. We were having a severe drought at the time and everything was terribly dry. I think he crawled into the bath looking for water. Oh dear, I'm sorry... I've made you start trembling again.'

She was conscious that his hands were now sliding down her bare arms, massaging them lightly, evenly, in a gentle circular motion. It was a most comforting sensation; mesmerising, in a way. She was sorry when after a while the gentle stroking ceased.

He tilted his head at her. His eyes were faintly teasing now. 'Surely you have Huntsmen spiders in Toorak? Or wherever it is that you live these days.'

'I live in South Melbourne. And yes, we do have the wretched things in Toorak *and* in South Melbourne. But I've never seen such an enormous one. Not that I've ever liked them, no matter what size they are,' she admitted. 'Whether they bite or not is immaterial to me. It's just the sight of them. Those great hairy legs ... and the way they appear without any warning.'

She shuddered involuntarily, and for a brief moment Simon's hands came to life again, moving over her bare flesh. ' "Huntsmen" seems too tame a word to describe them,' she added as his hands finally dropped away. 'I always think of them as tarantulas.'

'You get used to them,' Simon said with a shrug.

'*I* never would,' she said with feeling. As he stepped away from her, she felt herself flushing, conscious for the first time of her semi-nakedness, and the fact that her towel had slipped a bit, revealing far too much of one pearly breast. She jerked at the offending towel, hoping Simon wouldn't get the idea that she had enticed him into her bedroom deliberately, using the spider as a ploy. But he had felt her trembling ... he must know she had had no such thought in her mind.

'I'll leave you to have your shower.' Simon was already turning away. 'Just give a yell if you need me again.'

Did he mean something by that? Tanya wondered uneasily, as he strode, grinning, from the room. Was he letting her know that he would be a willing partner if she wished to invite him back ... to her bed next time?

She realised to her dismay that she was trembling again—only this time it had nothing to do with spiders or snakes. She was reliving the sensuous touch of his hands on her arms, the sensation of warmth as his palms massaged her bare skin, very conscious even now of the intimate brush of his fingertips, and the way her skin had tingled under his touch.

'Snap out of it, Tanya!' she said aloud, and after warily examining every corner of the shower recess she switched on the taps and stepped under the jet of steaming hot water.

If she had known what yet lay ahead of her that night, she would have stuffed her ears with cotton wool and buried her head in a pillow.

Just as she was finally drifting off to sleep, she was jolted wide awake by a loud thud, and the sound of heavy, creaking footsteps.

Something—or *someone*—was up on the roof!

She sat up abruptly, staring into the darkness, her eyes glassily alert. Whatever it was, it sounded far too heavy to be a bird...or a cat. It sounded heavy enough to be a tiger! Only there weren't any tigers in Australia—and even if there were, tigers didn't normally climb on to rooftops!

She felt the hairs lifting at the nape of her neck. What if it wasn't an animal at all, but a *human*? A *man*?

She chewed on her lip. What if it was a burglar trying to get in? Or an escaped convict? Were there any prison farms around here?

She ran her tongue over suddenly dry lips. Ought she to find Simon and warn him? He might not be able to hear the intruder from his room. Or he could be a sound sleeper.

She frowned into the darkness. There was an ominous silence above her now. She sat still, hardly breathing, her ears straining for the slightest sound. Could whoever was up there on the roof be listening too, afraid that he might have made too much noise, might have disturbed somebody in the house?

Or had he found what he had been looking for? A trapdoor in the roof? A skylight? An opening of some kind? Was he even now prising it open, preparing to climb down into the house?

She blew out her breath in a ragged sigh. Whoever or whatever was up there, she couldn't simply ignore it!

Reaching for her robe, she wrapped it around her and tiptoed from the room. Simon had mentioned that his room was the one at the far end of the house. It shouldn't be too hard to find...

He had left a light burning in the passage. Did that mean he hadn't yet retired for the night? Or had he left the light on in case she wanted—or *he* wanted——

She felt herself blushing furiously, and wished she had asked Simon's sister to come over for the night after all. She was beginning to realise that she wasn't nearly as cool-headed and in control of herself as she had always imagined she was.

She debated whether to go back to bed without disturbing Simon. But if those footsteps really did belong to an intruder, saying nothing could be putting them both at risk. Stifling her pride—and her qualms—she turned purposefully towards the door at the end of the passage. Then, sucking in her breath, she reached out, turned the handle, and pushed open the door.

The light from the passage shafted across the darkened room, its soft pearly glow falling across the bed in the middle of the room.

Tanya tilted her chin. This time, she decided, there will be no screaming, no dramatics. I'll just calmly go up to him and tell him what I heard.

She moved towards the bed, her bare feet making no sound on the woolly carpet. She could hear Simon's steady breathing, dimly see that he was lying on his back, his bare chest and arms exposed, the rest of his body a shadowy mound beneath the sheet that covered him.

She swallowed. Was the rest of him bare too? What if he leapt out of bed and——

She felt a nervous giggle rising in her throat. The laugh would be on him then, being caught in the state he'd caught her in earlier.

Or would it? Her face flamed suddenly, the giggle dying in her throat. With most men she knew, she would simply have laughed off a moment like that, uttered some flip remark, then tossed over a towel. With Simon Devlin she wasn't so sure she could be as cool as that. She remembered the touch of his hands earlier, as he had stroked her bare arms. It had been no more than an innocent gesture of comfort, and yet it had shaken her almost as much as that hideous spider.

Best to avoid any further intimate encounters with Simon Devlin. She didn't want to risk getting emotionally involved with him. Not that anything of the kind was likely to happen, with the differences, the antagonism between them. But emotions were funny things...

She stood poised beside the bed, beginning to wish she had ignored the footsteps on the roof and never come. Simon was fast asleep... If she slipped away now, he would never know she'd come.

But how could she leave a sleeping man and his house to the mercy of a possible intruder?

Before she could open her mouth to utter the cool words she had planned, before she could change her mind about saying anything at all and run for her life, she felt her arm being seized in a vice-like grip, and next moment she was yanked sideways, landing in a sprawled heap on the bed—literally on top of Simon Devlin!

She gasped as he wrapped his strong arms around her, clamping her to him. She could feel his warm breath on her cheek, was vividly aware of the steamy warmth of his naked body burning through the filmy layers that covered her. And then she heard his voice, very low, very soft. 'Well...I wasn't expecting this!'

And she panicked.

'Simon, let me go!'

Instead he gripped her more tightly, so that she could feel his thumping heartbeat against her own.

'Never look a gift horse in the mouth, don't they say?' he drawled, and pressed his mouth to hers, stifling the protest that rose, too late, to her lips.

She felt a curious lethargy flow over her as his lips moved over hers. While she was careful not to respond, she couldn't seem to pull away—not right away, at any rate. There was a mesmerising unreality about what was happening, about being in Simon Devlin's arms...in Simon Devlin's bed! It was like a half dream, half nightmare, part of her wanting him to go on kissing her, the other part knowing full well that it was the last thing in the world that she wanted.

And all the while there was an intruder creeping around the roof, trying to find a way in! Belatedly remembering that fact, and that that was why she was here, she tore her mouth away from his.

'Simon, for heaven's sake, what do you think you're doing? I came to tell you ——'

'Yes?' His voice was teasing, his face still so close to hers that she could feel his breath warming her skin—which she was uncomfortably aware felt more than warm enough already! 'What did you come to tell me?' he whispered. The shaft of light from the passage seemed to be shining more brightly now that her eyes had adjusted to the darkness, and in its glow she saw that Simon was grinning!

'I—I came to tell you there's someone on your roof!' She managed to get it out at last. Indignantly. Wanting to wipe that teasing smirk from his face.

'Someone on my roof?' He didn't sound at all alarmed. Already his lips were feeling for hers again, nibbling at the soft corners, and she heard a low chuckle in his throat. Angrily she jerked her head away. Didn't he care? Didn't he believe her? Surely he couldn't think——

She struggled to sit up, shaking back a silky lock of hair which had fallen across her eyes. By now she felt hot and dishevelled, and for the first time in her life she was also beginning to feel out of her depth, in a situation she wasn't sure she could handle.

It was crazy. Tanya Barrington simply never got herself into situations like this! Until now she had always managed to cope with any crisis that had arisen...especially where males were concerned. Where was her famed coolness now?

'So this is why they call you a tease and a breaker of hearts, is it?' Simon's tone was wry as his hands loosened their grip on her. 'I must say this is a new approach...it's quite novel.'

She stiffened, shocked. Was that what people were saying about her? She recalled that Nick Manning-Smith had recently hurled those very words at her after she had broken off with him. After she had refused to go to bed with him. Damn Nick, she thought. Damn all men! They only want one thing.

'I *did* hear someone,' she insisted, wondering why she didn't simply flounce away and leave Simon to deal with the intruder in any way he felt inclined. 'I heard footsteps on the roof. Don't you *care*? It could be anybody!'

'Any*body*?' Now he was quite openly laughing at her. She could see it in his eyes, hear it in his voice. Before she could stop him, he pulled her close again and buried his lips in the soft curve of her throat. 'It was only a possum,' he said, his voice muffled as his lips nuzzled into her warm skin. 'Don't worry, it can't get in.'

'A *possum*?' She tried to wriggle out of his arms, but he merely gave a soft chuckle and tightened his grip. She stifled a groan, knowing what he must be thinking, what he must be making of this bizarre little scene that *she* had instigated. The way he saw it, she had come voluntarily to his room, to his *bed*, on the flimsiest of pretexts, and as far as he was concerned, her reluctance now was sheer pretence, a coy little game she was playing, a game of hard-to-get, simply to titillate him further. Because she was a *tease*!

The thought gave her the strength to pull free at last, tugging herself from his grasp with a growl of exasperation, and rolling off the edge of the bed to land with a thump, in a most undignified fashion, on the floor.

Her face was flushed as she scrambled to her feet, scuffling out of his reach as he stretched out his arms to pull her back.

'You'd better get it into your head, Simon Devlin—I didn't come in here to play around, no matter what you might think. And you're the last man I'd want to play around *with*,' she spelt out savagely. 'If that was a possum I heard, OK, it was a possum. I'm sorry I woke you. I assure you it won't happen again.'

'Hey, wait!' He thrust aside the sheet that still partially covered him and swung his legs over the side of the bed. As his feet touched the floor she saw with relief that he was wearing shorts. And then, in alarm, that he was advancing towards her.

'Don't you come near me!' she shrilled, backing away. 'You have a highly inflated idea of your masculine appeal, Mr Devlin. It's entirely lost on me.'

He laughed, not wickedly, but with a sort of tolerant amusement. 'Will you calm down? I just want to talk to you.'

'Talk?' She paused, eyeing him warily.

'Look.' He spread his hands, appealing to her to be reasonable. 'When a beautiful girl wakes a fellow in the middle of the night, you can't blame him if he thinks he's got lucky.'

'Got *lucky*?' She screwed up her nose in distaste. 'How disgusting! You'd take any woman who threw herself at you, would you?'

'Not any woman, no. In your case, I was willing to play along. Surprised, but willing.'

Tanya flushed, because at one stage it must have looked as if she had been willing too. 'I came here for one reason and one reason only,' she snapped. 'You didn't give me a chance to explain. You just grabbed me. You're nothing but a—but an animal!' As she said it, an involuntary giggle bubbled inside her. She sounded like an outraged virgin! Which, if he only knew it, was precisely what she was!

'If I recall, you seemed to enjoy it too.'

That brought her up short. 'I did nothing of the kind!' She faced him indignantly. 'I—I was caught unawares. A girl doesn't expect to be manhandled when she comes on an errand of—of—— ' It was no good. 'Mercy'

sounded simply too histrionic. Laughter triumphed over
indignation, and she erupted into helpless giggles. 'This
is turning into a cheap melodrama!' she choked, wiping
her eyes with the back of her hand.

'Pure French farce,' Simon agreed. He, she saw, was
grinning too. Thank God they could laugh about it. How
could she have faced the rest of the weekend otherwise?

'Anyway,' she defended herself, choking back her
laughter, 'how was I to know it was only a possum? I
thought possums were light on their feet. Like cats.'

'They grow pretty big around here,' observed Simon,
'and they're a lot heavier on their feet than any cat.
Haven't you ever had possums climbing over your roof
at home? With all those big trees in Toorak, you must
have had plenty of possums when you lived there.'

'Sure. In our *trees*. But I never heard them on our
roof. We had a big two-storey place, well clear of any
trees.'

'Ah yes . . . of course.' There was a wealth of meaning
in that lazy 'of course'. The mention of her old two-
storey home had done it, and now the chip on his
shoulder was showing again, highlighting the differences that would always be there, like a gulf between
them, because he would never let her forget them. He
would always be ready to deride her more privileged upbringing, her easy ride through life.

'Well, since you're convinced it was a possum and not
an intruder,' she said crisply, 'I might as well go back
to bed.'

When she caught his quick grin, and saw him glance
pointedly towards his rumpled bed, she wished she had
expressed that a different way. Even more so when he
quipped, 'Be my guest.'

'Goodnight,' she said firmly, and moved purposefully towards the door.

'You'd better sleep in in the morning,' he called after her solicitously. 'We'll have breakfast at nine. I trust that's a civilised enough hour for you? There are a few things I want to do around the plantation before then. If you run into a strange woman in the kitchen, don't scream "intruder"—it'll only be Brigitte.'

Tanya flushed. He was never going to let her live to-night down, she could see that. 'Who's Brigitte?' she asked, pausing at the doorway. One of his country paramours? she wondered nastily.

'Brigitte is a local lass who pops in during the week to clean the place. And she helps me out at weekends when I have guests.'

And sometimes when you *don't* have guests? Tanya speculated cattily. Aloud, she said blandly, 'You're very fortunate. Having a sister who bakes cakes for you and a local girl who does everything else for you.' Let him make of 'everything else' what he will, she thought, with a sense of wicked satisfaction.

'I am indeed. Brigitte is a perfect gem…in every way.' He had guessed what was in her mind. She could tell by the mocking glimmer in his eyes. And he hadn't made any denials, she noticed.

Well, who cares? she thought, flashing him the sweetest smile she could muster as she swept from the room. He could have a whole bevy of adoring females for all she cared. Good luck to them. With Simon Devlin, they would need it!

CHAPTER FOUR

TANYA awoke to a blinding silvery sun in her eyes, and groaned. If she had remembered to draw the heavy curtains, she might have slept longer. Outside she could hear a cacophony of bird sounds. Early morning sounds. She glanced at her watch in dismay. Only seven-thirty—and breakfast wasn't until nine!

Well, she was awake now. She might as well get up and take a wander outside before breakfast. Simon no doubt was already out there somewhere, pottering around among his beloved trees.

She wasn't sure she was ready to face him again yet, but she had to do it some time, so it might as well be now as later. She would have to expect to be the butt of his jokes about spiders and possums, she guessed with a grimace, but that would be preferable to being reminded about other things that had happened last night—things she preferred not to think about, ever again.

She hoped Simon felt the same way, and didn't intend teasing her about those things as well. About the way she had lured him to her bedroom and let him catch her stark naked—her cheeks flamed at the memory... About the way she had later crept into *his* room in her flimsy night attire—and then wondered why he had grabbed her in a passionate embrace! It really had been her own fault . . . she should never have gone anywhere near his bed. Why hadn't she simply called out to him from the passage?

Because, she reasoned with a sigh, if there actually had been an intruder—and at the time she had genuinely believed that there might be—calling out to Simon could have alerted whoever was out there. So why cry over spilt milk? If Simon was going to have a field day over what had happened, she would just have to put up with it—and defend herself the best way she could. Or laugh it off. Yes, that was probably the best way to deal with it. Hadn't a bit of shared laughter diffused the situation last night?

She wandered across to the window and peered out. Amazingly, after last night's rain, there wasn't a cloud in the sky! The early March sun, although still low in the sky, would undoubtedly pack a punch later in the day. So much for worrying about packing sweaters and knee-high designer boots! Shorts and sandals would be the sensible thing to wear in this kind of weather.

Shorts? After last night's fiasco, exposing her long legs first thing in the morning to Simon Devlin's lascivious gaze would seem to be the height of folly. If the day turned out to be unbearably hot, and if the other guests were wearing shorts, she could always change later on. Right now, she settled on a compromise—lightweight trousers, a silk shirt, and sneakers.

As she dressed she let her gaze drift back to the window. Any distant view was blocked by scrubby-looking native shrubs, a few fruit trees of some kind, and a veritable jungle of tall spindly gum-trees—so unlike the graceful deciduous trees of the city and the lush English-style gardens of the type she had known so well at her old home.

She shrugged and turned away, unimpressed.

She wondered what the views were like from other rooms—from those long windows at the front of the house, for instance. Surely it wouldn't be more of the same? Acres and acres of dreary bush? Surely Simon would have done some landscaping, to add a bit of beauty to the place? She decided to take a look before venturing outside.

She felt a twinge of disappointment when she saw that it was indeed more of the same—gum-trees, wattles— none of which were in flower at this time of year—and a profusion of native shrubs she couldn't possibly have named. Where were the colourful flower beds? The roses, the camellias, the azaleas? Where were the sweeping green lawns? She couldn't see a blade of green grass anywhere! Only a depressing carpet of stubbly brown growth. Last night's rain seemed to have soaked into the earth and vanished without trace. The only evidence that there had been any rain at all were a few pearly drops glistening on the tips of the gum leaves.

Wistfully, her gaze followed the sweep of the driveway until it disappeared into the thicket of trees. In the far beyond she could see hills, dry and yellow and uninviting.

Where were Simon's tree plantations? she wondered without much interest. Somewhere to the rear of the property, hadn't he said? They would be out of sight from here.

'Oh!' said a voice, and she swung round to see a young woman—a veritable Amazon of a woman, tall, voluptuous and rosy-cheeked—halt in the doorway. Great brown eyes were regarding her curiously over a vase of freshly arranged flowers. They weren't, Tanya noted irrelevantly, the kind of flowers she was used to seeing at home in Toorak or South Melbourne. These were obviously native flowers of some kind—red brush-like flowers and large pale yellow flowers and clusters of white bell-like flowers amid wispy native greenery. The effect, she had to concede, was rather attractive. Where had the flowers sprung from? She wouldn't have thought there were any at all around here.

'You must be Miss Barrington,' said the Amazon woman, just as Tanya said,

'You must be Brigitte.'

They both laughed, and nodded, and Tanya was glad to see that there was no animosity in Brigitte's limpid brown eyes. The girl, if she *was* involved with Simon Devlin, must know that Tanya was no threat to her.

Tanya couldn't imagine the two *not* being involved. Brigitte was a real dish...and Simon, after all, was a free man, available, and right here on the spot whenever either of them wanted——

She snapped off the thought. If there was anything between them, it was no concern of hers. After all, it was no skin off her nose whether Simon Devlin had one woman or a hundred!

'Mr Devlin said you wouldn't be wanting your breakfast until nine.' Brigitte, looking apologetic now, even mildly distressed, put the vase down with a clatter. 'If you'll just give me a minute...'

Tanya was quick to reassure her. 'Nine o'clock will be fine, Brigitte. I thought I'd go out and explore a bit first. I was just getting my bearings,' she explained, waving a hand towards the windows. She was careful not to add, 'I'm going to look for Simon', and she also refrained from asking Brigitte if she knew where he was. She didn't want to antagonise her if she really was Simon's girl. Brigitte might take revenge by slipping some arsenic into her muesli!

The wicked thought brought a smile to her lips. Brigitte, if she only knew it, had no need to resort to such dramatic lengths. She would only have to slip a tarantula—or rather, a *Huntsman*—into her bed!

A shudder overtook her smile, and she left the room quickly. As she hastened away, she found herself conjuring up a vision of Brigitte and Simon Devlin as a couple. What an imposing twosome they would make— the voluptuous Amazon and the towering barrister from the bush! She couldn't imagine why the picture dampened her spirits rather than plucking another smile. It must have something to do with last night, she decided. Last night Simon Devlin had had his arms around *her*—and would have gone further if she'd let him. The man was a womaniser and an opportunist, and she hoped Brigitte was aware of the fact.

She left the house by a rear door, and came out into a slate-paved courtyard, shaded by overhanging grape-vines. Beyond the courtyard, sheltered on one side by a high stone wall, was a healthy-looking vegetable garden with an automatic watering system to keep it lush. Well, she thought approvingly, at least we can expect fresh salad vegetables for lunch!

She walked away from the house and pushed open a wire gate, making her way towards a plantation of young trees. She could see other plantations as well. Every-where, trees! Rows and rows of them, arranged in immaculate lines. They appeared to be of various species and at different stages of growth, and between each plantation there was a clearing, presumably for fire protection. One tree being very much like another to Tanya, she had no idea what kind of trees they were, other than that some were pine-trees and others eucalypts.

More hills rolled away behind, and further neat rows of more mature-looking trees were visible on the lower slopes. Her gaze flicked over the hills to the north-east— densely timbered hills, misty blue in the hazy morning sunlight.

She noticed one peak that was steeper and more rugged than the rest, with craggy overhangs of rock jutting from its heavily-wooded slopes. She wondered idly what it would be like to attempt to climb it. There didn't seem to be much else to do in this godforsaken place! There was no swimming pool, no tennis court, no real garden. What did one do for recreation in a spot like this? Particularly in the hot weather—and today was growing hotter and stickier by the minute. The nearest beach must be hundreds of miles away.

'Hi, there!'

She saw Simon waving to her from one of the plantations and she waved back, her heart giving a peculiar little jump. Was he going to tease her about last night or gallantly make no mention of it?

'Come over here!' he shouted.

He hadn't stopped giving her orders, she noticed, then she shrugged. Maybe she was being unfair. Maybe he was only trying to be friendly, to make her feel at home. Dim hope of that, she thought, grimacing. She had never felt so far from home in her life!

'I'm coming.' She didn't hurry. She didn't want to appear to be too eager for his company!

Simon was bending down examining a young tree when she reached him, but at her approach he straightened, drawing himself up to his full height.

Up close, out here in the raw bush, he looked bigger, tougher, more like the rough timber cutter's son than he had ever looked before. She heard herself gabbling,

'These trees must keep you busy. There are so many of them! I don't know how you find the time to run a property like this and run a law practice at the same time.'

'Well, I'm used to hard work,' he drawled, running a tanned hand through his rumpled brown hair.

'Meaning I'm not?' she flashed back, and when he glanced at her in surprise she felt like biting off her tongue. He hadn't been having a shot at her after all.

Simon grinned suddenly—and something caught in her throat. The sun was shining into his face, revealing every furrow, every line, every bone, and bringing his grey eyes to startling life. She had never seen him look so alive, or so...

She gulped. OK, so he had never looked so awesomely *masculine*. Ellie's word again! Well, she wasn't going to go into a flip about it. Let Brigitte do any flipping.

His shirt was open to the waist, revealing a disturbing amount of tanned flesh, and tantalising glimpses of dark curly hair. Last night he had held her in his arms and crushed her to that same chest, and she had felt the heat of his body flowing into her own. It all seemed unreal now, like a dream. A *bad* dream, she chided herself, and swung her gaze away.

'What are you doing?' she asked, pointing to the young tree he had been tending. It might be safer to stick to trees, even though she felt woefully ignorant on that particular subject.

He explained that he was doing a bit of reshaping, which was important in the case of these young Douglas firs because they were being produced for the Christmas tree market. He went on to identify some of the other trees he had planted, reeling off names like radiata pine and Norway spruce and mountain ash, and confiding that one day he intended to produce a small plantation of western red cedar for the specialist furniture market.

Most of the names meant little or nothing to Tanya, and his words washed over her without fully seeping in. She felt way out of her depth here in Simon's forest, among his obviously much-loved trees. She felt ignorant and alien and uninvolved, and that made her feel restless and uncomfortable. She was used to feeling on top of things, to knowing what she was doing and what she was talking about, and here in these foreign surroundings she felt all at sea. She cast about for a diversion.

'Have you ever climbed that mountain, Simon?' she asked, pointing to the rugged peak she had noticed before. 'It would be quite a challenge, I would think.'

He tilted his head at her. 'What's this? Miss Barrington's latest whim? Mountain climbing?'

'Whim?' Her blue eyes glittered like sapphires. 'What do you mean—my latest whim?'

'I seem to recall another whim of yours. To hang-glide from Melbourne's tallest building and glide across the Yarra River. You were arrested, though, before you could jump. Of course, you made sure first that the cameras were rolling. It made quite a splash in the press, I remember. "Judge's daughter arrested in city hang-gliding attempt." Yes, it was quite a headline-catcher.'

She reddened, because there was a good deal of truth in what he said. But even the guilty, she thought, rallying, are permitted a defence.

'You're throwing something up at me that happened when I was still at university. It was a stupid prank—I was much younger and sillier then. And you're conveniently forgetting that there were three others besides me. I got all the publicity, though, because I happened to be Justice Barrington's daughter. Having a well-known judge for a father isn't all roses,' she said tartly.

'Go on . . . you lapped up all the publicity. That was all you were looking for. You never intended to jump. It was just a publicity stunt.'

'We *did* intend to jump,' Tanya denied swiftly. 'And we would have too, if one of the others hadn't alerted the media—and if one of the cameramen hadn't in turn alerted the security guards. He was worried about our safety, he told us later.'

And maybe he had been wise to stop them, she acknowledged now, in hindsight. It had been a pretty stupid thing to attempt. Stupid and dangerous. At the time, she—and the others too, she suspected—hadn't thought of it as anything but a bit of harmless fun, a way of letting off steam after a hard year of study, and a way of showing what they could do. They had all been proficient hang-gliders. It had been the fad among her crowd that year.

'Well, thank goodness someone had a bit of sense,' Simon muttered, referring to the cameraman, not to her. He glanced at his watch. 'Time to head back for breakfast. Brigitte will get jumpy if we're late. She's cooking us a hot breakfast.'

Because she was still peeved with him for accusing her of being a publicity-seeker, Tanya rashly decided to go on the attack herself. 'I see what you mean about Brigitte being a gem,' she said in honeyed tones. 'She's gorgeous. A man like you must find her irresistible.'

'A man like me?' The gleam in his eye wasn't solely from the sun. Was he laughing at her, or was he angry? She couldn't tell which.

She didn't want to get into a discussion about the kind of man he was, because that would mean bringing up what had happened last night, and that was the last thing she wanted to do. So she merely waved an airy hand and said silkily, 'I should imagine any warm-blooded male would find Brigitte irresistible. She's some woman!' With that, she turned her back on him, and started trudging back towards the house. She heard Simon closing the gap between them, and then his voice at her ear, mocking her.

'She is at that. But any warm-blooded male would find her irresistible at his peril. Brigitte's husband is six feet five and the local wood-chopping champion.'

Tanya's head snapped around. Brigitte was *married*? She felt like kicking herself. Why hadn't she looked for a wedding ring? She could have saved herself Simon's taunts. To retrieve the situation, she resorted to some mockery of her own, determined to have the last word.

'Oh, bad luck,' she commiserated, and deliberately quickened her pace. She was aware as she neared the house that her heart felt inexplicably lighter. Surely it couldn't have anything to do with the fact that the statuesque Brigitte was married? That didn't change anything. Simon Devlin was still a womaniser, and she still didn't want him pawing *her*.

Pawing her? Her mind flitted back to last night. Last night she had not, she recalled with a flush, looked on what Simon was doing to her as *pawing*. Pawing was something she found repugnant, and Simon's embrace had not been repugnant. Although she hadn't sought it or encouraged it or visibly responded to it, she did recall feeling a stir of *something*—something she had never felt before, not even with Nick Manning-Smith. What she had felt for Nick at one time had been more hero-worship than real attraction, whereas what she had felt last night had been...

'Lust,' she breathed, pleased that she could explain the emotion away. She had had her first real stirrings of animal lust. And she had dared to call Simon an animal! The thought brought a self-mocking smile. Ironic, that she should lust after a man she didn't even like! Yes, she was no better than an animal... 'Or a man,' she muttered.

'Sorry?'

She turned sharply to see Simon eyeing her speculatively, and at once felt a prickle of heat along her cheekbones. Heaven forbid, if he could read minds! She had better watch herself. Whatever she had felt last night she had better make sure she never felt again. Lust, she had heard, could often deepen into something else— helpless infatuation, even love...and think how vulnerable she would be then!

She didn't fancy being vulnerable to a man like Simon Devlin. He would trample all over her, make impossible demands on her, and then toss her aside when he grew tired of her. Even if he didn't grow tired of her, even if he developed some real feeling for her, how could anything ever come of it? He loved the bush and loathed living in the city. She loved the city and loathed everything about the bush. Besides which, they barely had a thing in common!

'Just humming a tune,' she said with a shrug.

'I'm glad your bush surroundings and this crystal-clear mountain air are making you feel happy,' said Simon, and she noted the dryness of his tone. He wasn't fooled for a minute! He knew perfectly well that she wasn't happy here, that she didn't fit in, that she wasn't even interested in trying to fit in. And he was hardly likely to lose any sleep over it!

At the thought of him losing his sleep, Tanya blushed, and at the same time felt a reluctant giggle—of hysteria?—rising to her throat. Was she forever going to be reminded of last night?

Surprisingly, she managed to relax over breakfast. Brigitte bustled around, thrusting hot scrambled eggs, crisp fried bacon and grilled herbed tomatoes under their noses, along with buttered toast, freshly squeezed orange juice and lemon tea. Tanya was now acutely aware of the gold band on Brigitte's left hand, and wondered how she could have missed it before. She hoped Simon hadn't put her bantering remarks earlier down to jealousy. Heaven forbid!

Well, from now on, she decided, she was going to be thoroughly aloof, thoroughly dispassionate. That should soon disabuse him of any such idea!

So when, after breakfast, Simon summoned her to his study to discuss their coming trial, she managed to be coolly professional and briskly businesslike, and she sensed that even the hard-to-please Mr Devlin was impressed by the efficiency with which she had prepared her case. Did he still suspect that someone was helping her? she wondered, recalling with a surge of indignation the accusation he had made the other day. She wouldn't be surprised!

By the time they wound up their conference, it was nearly lunchtime. The other guests, Tanya thought in relief, ought to be arriving any time now. She would welcome some moral support!

'I'd better go and change,' she said quickly, rising from her chair. Simon had already changed out of his rough work clothes and heavy boots, exchanging them when he came in for a clean white shirt, hip-hugging blue jeans and comfortable loafers.

She saw his eyes make a lazy sweep over her still immaculate slacks and raw silk blouse. 'What were you thinking of changing into?' he asked, his tone sardonic. 'Jeans, T-shirt and boots? You've decided to rough it a bit?'

'I was thinking of a skirt—or a sun-dress,' she said evenly, only just remembering her vow of cool indifference, and refraining from snapping at him.

He gave a brief laugh. 'Please yourself, but I fail to see what's wrong with what you have on now.'

'It's too hot for trousers,' Tanya tilted her chin. 'A sun-dress will be cooler. And I'll feel fresher.'

He shrugged. 'Your decision. You'll only have to change again after lunch if you intend to go tramping through the plantation with the others. Or if you want to go swimming...'

'Swimming?' Tanya brightened. 'I didn't see a pool.'

'No, but there's a river.'

'You swim in the *river*?' She barely repressed a shudder. Visions of slime, reeds, and hidden snags rose in her mind.

Simon nodded, his eyes derisive. 'There's a natural rock pool where the water is deep and clear and ideal for swimming.'

She shrugged, not knowing whether to believe him.

'Tomorrow we'll do some bushwalking...' There was a taunting note in Simon's voice as he drawled the word 'bushwalking,' as if he expected her to be incapable of such exertion. If he only knew how often she had tramped over snow-covered mountains on her numerous ski-trips, both here in Australia and on the ski-slopes of

New Zealand and Europe, he wouldn't be so ready to mock her!

Before she could form a retort, the crunching sound of tyres on gravel announced their first arrival. 'Too late to change now,' Simon said impassively, and she wondered if he had deliberately kept her talking so that she wouldn't have time. 'Come on, let's go and meet whoever it is.'

It was Joe Camillieri from Sanctuary House, and his quiet, flaxen-haired fiancée Amanda Scott. Both greeted Tanya warmly, as if they were genuinely pleased to meet her—or in Joe's case, to see her again.

It was later, as they were sipping ice-cold drinks in the relative coolness of the vine-covered patio at the side of the house, that Simon's final luncheon guest, Dimity Donohue, the local magistrate, arrived.

Tanya looked her over curiously as Simon introduced her around. She looked to be in her early to mid-thirties—about Simon's age, she hazarded. An attractive woman with sleek dark hair, intense brown eyes, and a forceful, self-assured manner. A woman of strong opinions—an opinion on everything, Tanya quickly discovered. She must be impressive on the magistrate's bench, Tanya mused, wondering what Simon thought of her.

Simon treated her with a politeness and a respect he'd rarely shown his briefing solicitor, she noted sourly. But she was damned if she was going to speculate on his relationship with the woman. Simon's women were welcome to him!

She sat back, a faint smile on her lips, hoping that now there were others around, the weekend would take an upward swing. With other guests for Simon to direct his attention to—and he *was*, she thought waspishly, listening to him engaging in a lively exchange with Dimity Donohue on the merits of the new Crime Act—and with other company to divert *her*, perhaps she might even end up enjoying herself. She might even learn something, if she listened carefully enough to the exchanges flying back and forth between Simon and Dimity. And that was one of the reasons she was here, wasn't it? To learn all she could.

It was a congenial lunch, congenial company. The others, Tanya had to own with some surprise, were rather a pleasant change from her usual circle of friends, who could be pretty smug and self-centred at times, with their preoccupation with money and position and the high life and their smart, often thoughtlessly cruel repartee. Joe and Amanda, and even Dimity in her own way, impressed her as being far less self-seeking, less materialistic, less absorbed with their own egos, showing more concern for others, for the environment, for the disadvantaged in the community, for all kinds of issues that her high-flying friends would never be bothered with. Tanya joined in the various discussions with enthusiasm.

Soon after lunch, Dimity excused herself, catching Simon's hand as she explained, 'I have to go into Warragul and check on the arrangements for tonight. I want to make sure they're being carried out properly,' she added in a tone that boded ill for somebody, Tanya suspected, if they weren't. 'See you tonight.' She was still looking at Simon in particular as she made her farewell.

So there *is* something between them, Tanya thought—and despite her determination not to speculate or care a damn about Simon's women friends, she felt an odd little twinge at the thought. If she hadn't known better, she would have said it was a twinge of jealousy. But that was idiotic. Laughable.

And so, if it wasn't jealousy, what was it? Home-sickness? That must be it. She was missing town, missing her friends, missing the social activities she would have been indulging in at this moment if Simon Devlin hadn't persuaded her—*forced* her wasn't too strong a word—to come up here into this remote, uninviting part of the world for the weekend. If she felt a bit down, she could lay the feeling squarely at Simon Devlin's feet! Dimity Donohue had nothing to do with it.

After Dimity had left, Simon took Joe, Amanda and Tanya for a tour of his extensive tree plantation, and Tanya thought with a listless sigh that if she were back in town she could have been playing tennis right now. She noticed that Amanda wasn't showing much interest in the trees either. When the girl heard Simon mention his rock pool, her pale blue eyes lit up.

'Let's go for a swim! It's so hot. There's time, isn't there, Simon, for a cool dip?'

Simon spread his hands. 'Be my guest.'

They headed back to the house to change into swimming gear. Tanya had brought only a bikini, not a one-piece swimsuit with her, and, feeling rather exposed with only a towel for cover, she slipped a sun-dress on over her skimpy bikini, before thrusting her feet into open sandals. She was by no means certain that she was going swimming yet. Simon could have been exagger-ating the river's clarity and freshness. She preferred to see for herself first.

When she rejoined Amanda where they had arranged to meet outside, she glanced around for the two men. There was no sign of either of them.

'They've gone on ahead,' Amanda told her. She too was covered up, Tanya noted, in a cotton throw-over. 'Simon said to just follow that gravelly path over there down to the river.' She pointed, and Tanya saw a path winding down the slope, with thick bushland on one side and fruit trees sprouting from the dry grass on the other. 'Simon said if we stick to the path we'll be all right,' Amanda added, screwing up her face in a brief grin. 'As if we're going to get lost!'

That would be about all I need—to get lost in the bush, Tanya thought as they set off. She realised she was looking forward to having a swim now. The sun was high in the sky, and meltingly hot. The air seemed to shimmer with the heat, and there wasn't a breath of wind.

The path was wide enough for two to walk comfortably side by side. They followed its meandering course down the slope, unable to see Simon and Joe as yet because of the thick scrub ahead.

'Those apples look enticing.' Tanya's eyes lit up as she noticed the shiny red fruit hanging from the branches of one of the fruit trees off to their right. 'Want one?'

'Sure,' said Amanda, but she made no attempt to follow when Tanya swung off the path into the dry straggly grass. 'Be careful of snakes,' she warned.

'I will,' Tanya called back. She hadn't even thought of snakes until Amanda's reminder, but now, heeding the warning, she began to tread more gingerly, creeping as carefully, as quietly as she could through the thick grass in the mistaken belief that that was the best way to avoid disturbing any snakes in the vicinity.

She heard a rustling sound in the grass, and with her heart in her mouth, she paused. Was it simply a bird fossicking in the grass? Surely it must be! She took a cautious step forward, and hearing no further sounds, reached out to pluck an apple from the nearest tree.

What happened next brought a gasp to her lips and almost knocked the breath from her body. She was dimly aware of a different kind of rustling from somewhere behind her, then her legs were whisked from beneath her and her whole body was swept up into the air. Gasping, she found herself clasped in strong, none-too-gentle arms, looking up into Simon Devlin's thunderous face.

'You damned fool, *what the hell do you think you're doing*?'

She couldn't find her voice for a moment—she was too stunned. When she did find it, she heard herself demanding in a high-pitched, rather shaky voice, trying to make a joke of it, 'Are your apples forbidden fruit, then? You should have told me.'

'You ignorant, stupid little bitch!' he roared at her. 'I don't care about the apples—I was thinking of *snakes*, damn you! Don't you know you never walk barelegged through thick dry grass? And wearing open sandals, for heaven's sake! I know you're a dyed-in-the-wool city girl, but don't you know *anything*?'

Shaken, she shouted back, 'I *was* being careful! I was hardly making a sound.'

Simon groaned, and in two long strides had her back on the path, roughly setting her down beside a wide-eyed Amanda, and releasing her abruptly as if she were more repulsive to him than the snakes he was warning her about. Joe, Tanya was dimly aware, was there too, looking on with mild concern in his dark eyes.

But Simon hadn't finished with her yet. Towering over her, his eyes flailing her, he rasped, 'For pity's sake, Tanya, you don't *creep* through dry grass!' His tone was pitying. 'You make as much noise as you can, so that any snakes in the vicinity can hear you coming—or rather feel your vibrations, since they're deaf—and can slither out of your way. And you always, always wear long pants and boots—or sturdy shoes—in snake country.'

'Well, *you're* not,' she accused, eyeing his bare legs—and despite herself, noting how well-shaped, how strong and powerfully masculine they were. Like everything else about him.

'I wasn't planning on leaving the path, was I?' he said scathingly. 'I had no choice. At least I'm wearing shoes that give me a bit of protection. And *I* made plenty of noise.'

'Why didn't you just shout out to me—I'd have gone back to the path straight away.' She faced him, chin thrust out, hands on hips, his belligerent attitude making her disinclined to thank him—yet.

'You might not have *made* it back,' he said brutally. 'Didn't you hear any rustling in the grass? This fruit orchard is alive with snakes!'

Tanya turned pale. 'I thought it was birds. Well, how was I to know?' she demanded, rallying. 'I haven't been brought up in the bush as you have. I've never even *seen* a snake—except in zoos and sanctuaries—let alone heard one.'

'Well, you'll know next time, won't you?' Simon said harshly.

Their eyes clashed, the glint of cold pewter in his, the spark of glittering sapphire in hers. 'I seem to have lost my desire for a swim,' she said with a toss of her head. 'I think I'll go back to the house and change into something more suitable for this wild bushland of yours,' she snarled at him. 'Nobody warned me how dangerous it was going to be. I think I need a nice long drink. It might fortify me for whatever lies ahead.'

'I think we could all do with a drink,' said Amanda, grabbing her arm with an alacrity that suggested she wasn't any more at home in the bush than Tanya. 'Let's forget about our dip in the river. Snakes can swim, you know,' she confided to Tanya, who shivered, and nodded. 'Come on, Joe. Coming, Simon?'

'Sure. Why not?' There was a resigned note in Simon's voice now, his knitted brow the only remaining sign— the only *visible* sign—of his former wrath.

He'll be pleased to see the last of the lot of us, Tanya brooded. Especially me.

CHAPTER FIVE

IT WAS a twenty-minute drive into Warragul from Simon's place. Mercifully, the atmosphere between Tanya and Simon had relaxed considerably since their clash earlier in the afternoon. Tanya had taken Simon aside before getting into the car, and had thanked him for what he had done for her, admitting that she had been foolish to venture into the apple orchard without taking proper precautions, and assuring him that she had learnt a good lesson and would know better next time.

She had realised with hindsight that Simon's angry reaction had been fully justified—she could easily have been bitten by a venomous snake and might have been languishing in hospital by now, or worse—and she ought to be grateful to him for snatching her out of a dangerous situation, regardless of his own safety.

Luckily, Simon was holding no grudges. 'I'm glad we didn't have to cart you off to hospital,' was his languid response, his lips curving into a smile. He was so attractive, she thought, when he smiled. If only he would smile more often! 'I'm sure you'd have loved being stuck in a hospital for days on end.'

'What's wrong with hospitals?' she had quipped, relieved that he wasn't making it difficult for her. 'I was in hospital once, you know, and the nursing staff were wonderful—they really pampered me the whole time I was there.'

'One of Melbourne's top private hospitals, no doubt.' Simon's tone was faintly caustic now, and Tanya wished she'd kept her mouth shut. 'Not a struggling country hospital like the one we have out here. You may not have found that one so appealing. Having to share a room with roughnecks from the bush. Cared for by overworked nurses with no time for pampering.'

She felt a stir of irritation because his remarks had reminded her again of the differences between them. But she managed to stifle the feeling. Having cleared the air, she wanted to keep it that way. 'I'd have managed,' was all she said, and they left it at that.

Tonight she was wearing a deceptively simple cream dress and stylish Italian shoes and a string of pearls that her parents had given her for her twenty-first birthday. She had been brought up to look for quality in her clothes, but she shopped wisely and didn't squander her money.

She had noticed Simon's brow shoot up earlier as his gaze had flicked over her, as if he were assessing the total cost. The shoes, admittedly, were a top brand, but she had bought them at a sale, besides which she had always found Italian shoes to be hard-wearing and deliciously comfortable. And her dress had been a good investment—well worth the little extra she had had to pay for it. It was well cut and versatile and looked as good as it felt.

But what would be the good of explaining any of that to Simon Devlin? He had already made up his mind about her.

The dinner was held in the Warragul civic centre. Most of the invited guests were local lawyers, policemen, or in some way connected with the law. Dimity Donohue swept over to greet them on their arrival, leading them to the head table and waving Simon into the seat next to hers, with the other speaker for the evening, a police inspector called Ian Meadows, on her other side. Dimity placed Tanya between Ian Meadows and Joe Camillieri, several places away from Simon. She wants him to herself, Tanya thought. Well, good luck to her.

During dinner, Dimity kept the conversation rolling, directing most of her remarks, and her attention, to Simon. Simon didn't seem to mind. He treated her with the same courtesy he had at lunchtime, smiling easily and often, while at the same time, unlike Dimity, attempting to draw the others into the conversation.

When the meal was over it was Dimity who leapt up to introduce the first speaker for the evening, Ian Meadows, while Simon's speech followed later, Dimity announcing Simon as if he was the one everyone had been waiting to hear. Tanya thought with a wry smile that the woman only needed a roll of drums to make her introduction complete.

Both talks were interesting and informative, though Simon's speech, because of his wonderful voice and resonance, and with his barrister's training, was the more riveting of the two. He even brought humour into it, which wasn't easy, since he was talking about amendments to the Crime Act. It was with the deftest of touches that he cleverly brought in snatches of humour to lighten the topic and keep his audience enthralled.

There was no doubt about it, Tanya mused, Simon Devlin was a powerhouse of charm, knowledge, wit, and—yes, damn it, sex appeal. It flowed out of him, creating an aura that spread its mesmerising effect over the entire hall. You had to admire him ... be entranced by him. Surely nobody, she thought, could be indifferent to him.

Of course, *privately* he had a less attractive side, a far less admirable side, and most of the people here would never see that side of him. But *she* had seen it...the autocratic, sneering, antagonistic bushman with the giant-sized chip on his shoulder when it came to people who'd had privileges he had never had. And infuriatingly, he stubbornly refused to look beyond those shallow surface trappings to the real person lying behind.

She knew that she was thinking of herself, and felt herself flushing. Would she really *want* him to get to know her better? Would she, for that matter, want to get to know *him* better? It could well be dabbling with dynamite, getting close to Simon Devlin.

Simon came back to the table amid thunderous applause, with Dimity's effusive words of thanks still ringing in Tanya's ears. The magistrate's vote of thanks to Ian Meadows had been lukewarm by comparison.

The evening wound up quickly after that, and when the four of them took their leave of Dimity Tanya noted that the magistrate barely had eyes for anyone but Simon, and she even reached up and kissed him on the lips—startling him or pleasing him, Tanya couldn't tell which—as she thanked him again for his speech. She made no attempt to kiss Ian Meadows, Tanya noticed.

She wondered if Simon was sorry he had house guests for the night. If he hadn't, would he have driven Dimity home? Or taken her to *his* home? Tanya had no doubt that Dimity would have agreed to anything he suggested!

With a blush she recalled how eagerly, how willingly, Simon had leapt to take advantage of *her* last night, when he had thought she was offering herself to him—a girl he barely knew or liked! So how much more eager and willing he must be to get the panting, desirable Dimity into his bed!

Well, one thing was for sure. There was going to be no repeat of last night! If there was going to be any nocturnal wandering tonight, Tanya resolved, it would have to be between Joe's room and Amanda's. She, Tanya, would have to hear an intruder actually falling through the roof before she would budge from her bed tonight!

In fact, something did rouse her from her sleep in the middle of the night. Or in the early hours of the morning... she wasn't sure which. She was dimly aware of a telephone ringing.

When it stopped, she lay still, biting her lip. For a moment all she could hear was the beating of her own heart. Who would be ringing at this hour? Then she heard a faint scuffling sound in the passage. Who was out there? What was going on? She was determined that this time she wasn't going to go rushing out. She certainly wasn't going to go rushing to Simon!

Then she must have drifted back to sleep, because the next thing she knew, it was daylight, and the sun was already well up. She looked in dismay at her watch. Nearly nine o'clock already!

She splashed her face with warm water, ran a comb through her hair, and threw on a pair of jeans and a shirt. Brigitte would be upset if she kept her waiting, assuming the girl had prepared a hot breakfast again this morning.

But there was no sign of Brigitte in the kitchen this morning. Only Simon was there, briskly stirring eggs in a bowl, when she burst into the kitchen, her face still flushed from her sleep.

There was no sign of Joe or Amanda either.

'I'm glad I'm not the last one up,' she said in relief.

Simon turned to her, his expression whimsical. 'Oh, but you are. Joe and Amanda have already gone.'

'Gone?' Tanya looked at him blankly. 'What do you mean, gone? For a walk, you mean?'

'No, I mean they've gone back to town.' He stopped stirring for a moment. 'Amanda had a call in the night to say that her father had suffered a heart attack. Joe's taken her home.'

'Oh.' That left her alone with Simon for the rest of the day! 'I could have driven back to Melbourne with them,' she said, faintly piqued that Simon hadn't given her the opportunity.

'What, at four in the morning?' Simon's eyes were derisive. 'Are you so anxious to get back to your precious city?'

She didn't answer that. How could she deny it? She felt like a fish out of water out here in the bush. Instead, she said with a shrug, 'You must have so much work you want to do. I'll only get in your way.'

He moved across to the stove. 'I've been up working since dawn. I'm prepared to take a few hours off to give you your wish.'

'My wish?' Her eyes brightened. Did he intend to drive her back to town after breakfast?

'Would you mind popping the bread in the toaster?' he asked as he poured the beaten eggs into a saucepan and started stirring them over the heat. She waited, holding her breath. When his answer came, it was all she could do not to expel her breath in an audible gasp.

'You expressed a desire to go climbing,' Simon said pleasantly. 'An excellent idea. Good healthy exercise, fresh mountain air, and a bit of a challenge thrown in...'

She carefully hid her dismay. Had she really said that?

'Why not?' she tossed back. If he expected her to cry off, to cave in, he didn't know Tanya Barrington! She was damned if she was going to show any reluctance, any trepidation whatsoever.

'We'll have a picnic lunch,' Simon decided amiably as they ate their scrambled eggs. 'Oh, and by the way—we won't be climbing that rocky hill behind the house. I have a far more fascinating climb in mind.'

'Mm?' She eyed him uncertainly. Did that glint in his eye mean anything in particular?

'We'll go up into the Baw Baws,' he said, rising to fetch the coffee pot.

'You mean—the Baw Baw Mountains? As in Mount Baw Baw, where people go skiing in the winter?' She looked at him in surprise. 'Are they within walking distance of here?'

He shook his head. 'We'll have to take the four-wheel-drive to the start of the walking track. Be prepared for a fairly vigorous climb. But we should be back well before nightfall.' His teeth glinted in a quick smile.

The smile on the face of a tiger, she thought, her stomach doing a funny little looping dive. 'Is this a test of some kind?' she asked levelly. 'A test of my endurance?'

He laughed aloud at that, a short, taunting laugh that did nothing to allay her qualms. 'Merely giving you your wish. It's a beautiful part of the world...one should never come up this way and not see it. You'll need to wear boots and jeans, and take a sweater for later. I can lend you a hat, if you want one.'

'No, thanks. I won't need one.' If the sun was over-bright, her sun-glasses would be all she would need.

'Please yourself.'

They parted after breakfast to go and change, and when they met up again, she saw his face darken.

'For God's sake, Tanya, I meant real boots, not those high-heeled designer things! Do you want to twist an ankle? Haven't you brought any sturdy shoes with you?'

She shook her head. 'Only sneakers. They're very strong and comfortable, though,' she assured him hastily.

'Go and put them on.'

When she came back he handed her a knapsack, packed with a few light provisions, to carry on her back. He, she noticed, was carrying a bulkier one.

It was another glorious day, with hardly a cloud in the sky. The drive into the mountain country was picturesque and at times hair-raising. The road was steep, rough, and frighteningly narrow, the bends treacherous, the drop over the edge of the ridge heart-stopping. But the views across the deep rugged valleys, when she was game enough to look down, were spectacular.

When they reached the start of the walking track, they left the vehicle parked under a clump of stringybarks and set off on foot. Tanya's nostrils quivered at the damp, tangy aroma rising from the lacy ferns in the gullies, her ears buzzed to the tumultuous chirruping and chirping in the trees, and she reached for her sun-glasses to shade her eyes as the sun blazed down on gently cascading waterfalls and glistening rock-faces.

Their feet made barely a sound on the damp forest floor as they trudged on uphill through forests of mountain ash, each giant tree rising straight as the mast of a ship, without a branch or any perceptible diminution of girth almost as far as the eye could see.

'You're standing among some of the tallest trees in the world,' Simon told her, and Tanya, feeling dwarfed, looked up in awe.

'Touch them,' he urged. 'Here... this one. Put your arm round its trunk. Feel its strength, its vitality. This one would be more than a hundred years old.'

Tanya tentatively touched the smooth trunk of the giant tree with the palm of her hand. She reached up to feel the texture of the bark which clung to the trunk in long strips. And then, with a shrug, she stretched out her arms and embraced the sturdy trunk, pressing her body against the tree, with her bare cheek resting against the roughened bark.

'If anyone had told me I'd be hugging a tree one day, I'd have laughed in their face,' she said out of the side of her mouth. But it was true—this was the way to feel the tree's strength, its solidity. She could even, in some mysterious way, sense its vitality, its life-force, throbbing under her touch. Pure imagination, of course... surely? A tree was just a tree.

'You felt it, didn't you?' Simon asked quietly as she stepped away, rubbing her cheek. Still faintly bemused, she glanced up at him, and for a second she found her gaze caught in his. She had a fleeting impression of pleasure, of surprise, before he broke the contact and swung back on to the path. She followed, the vibrant touch of the giant mountain ash still vividly with her.

The climb was becoming steeper and the air up here was clear and crisp. At times the silence of the forest was splintered by the cackling laugh of a kookaburra, or the *thrump*, *thrump* of a wallaby in a hurry to get out of their way. It was rough going, hard on the leg muscles. After a while Tanya had to stop again to catch her breath.

Simon was watching her, she noticed...a taunting glint to his eye. He *is* testing me, she thought indignantly. He wants to find out what I'm made of, how long I can stick with it, keep up.

But Simon said nothing, merely pointing out other trees as they climbed higher—manna gums, mountain greys, black and blue peppermints, myrtles, stands of introduced blue-gums. The names spun round in Tanya's head. How could anyone ever remember them all?

It was hot work, toiling up the mountainside. The sun was beating down from high in the sky, and Tanya reached up to mop her brow, pushing her damp hair from her eyes. Damn him, he was right—she should have worn a hat. She realised that her legs were aching, that they felt like lead. She wondered if they would hold out.

'Nearly there.' Simon was watching her again, she realised. He was worried, no doubt, that she wasn't going to make it. If she didn't, how he would crow at her lack of stamina!

'Nearly *where*?' she asked, glancing round. The path had for some time been growing rockier, steeper, and more perilous. She had lost all sense of direction. All she knew was that they were somewhere in the heart of the Baw Baw Mountains, miles from their car—miles from anywhere!

'You mean another waterfall?' she hazarded. She'd settle for a flat rock and a ten-minute rest!

'You'll see. Watch your footing, it's steep here.'

'I am,' she said fervently. She didn't fancy sliding down into the timbered ravine below. The view though from up here was breathtaking.

'There!' With a flourish, Simon stood aside so that she could see past him.

It had appeared out of nowhere—a small, quaint timber hut, perched on a flat ridge of rock, with an outcrop of moss-covered rocks sheltering it from above.

'Does it belong to you?' she asked, her eyes lighting up. A place to rest at last!

Simon shook his head. 'It's for anyone who comes up here. There are huts like this dotted around most of the mountain tracks. They provide a safe haven if you happen to get caught in a snowstorm, or a sudden downpour, or for any other reason. In our case, it'll be a good place to stop and have lunch.'

'I thought you'd never ask,' Tanya said thankfully.

Inside, the sturdy little hut had a welcoming air. It was immaculately clean, with everything neatly in its place. The functional chairs and table had, like the hut itself, been fashioned from snow-gum logs. As had the narrow bed in one corner. Tanya's mouth tightened when she saw it. If Simon Devlin thought...

She sucked in a deep breath. If he tried anything up here, he'd regret it!

There was also a fireplace, a drip-safe for storing perishables, and even some neatly-folded blankets. Blankets...for the bed? She groaned inwardly. What had she got herself into?

Simon was already burrowing into his knapsack. Tanya's eyes opened wide when he drew out a bottle of Moët et Chandon champagne wrapped in a plastic ice-pack, and two champagne glasses.

'A toast, I think, would be appropriate,' he said, popping the cork. He poured, and handed her a glass. 'To a successful climb!'

She raised her glass, wondering ruefully if she would have seen any champagne if she had failed to make it to the top.

'A successful climb,' she echoed, and beamed suddenly, feeling she had achieved a victory of sorts. He hadn't expected her to make it!

As their eyes met over their clinking glasses, she saw a new glowing softness in his. It would not be for her, though, she realised with a vague sense of disappointment. It would be for his beloved forest world.

'You love it up here, don't you, Simon?' she asked quietly. 'I don't mean just here...in these mountains. I mean the bush, the forest, your home...'

Something stirred deep down in the grey depths. There was a long pause before he answered.

'Yes, I love it up here. I always have. It gets into your blood...it stirs your senses...it keeps you feeling alive.'

'I suppose you have to be born here to feel like that,' Tanya said pensively—and flushed, hoping he wouldn't get the idea that *she* would ever want to fall in love with the place.

'Not necessarily,' Simon answered, eyeing her speculatively. 'There's a magic out here that can grow on anybody, at any time...' His eyes narrowed imperceptibly, as if he were trying to ascertain if any of the magic had as yet rubbed off on *her*.

She had better disabuse of that idea him right here and now!

'I'm starving...is there anything to eat?' Let him think that, to her, food for the body was more important than food for the soul. It was vital that she keep at a safe distance from Simon Devlin—not get any closer! Let him despise her if that would keep her safe from him.

'Sandwiches coming up.' If he was disappointed in her, he wasn't showing it. Of course, he wouldn't want to get any closer to her either. They were too many poles apart. They lived in different worlds, preferred different lifestyles, wanted different things from life. To get any closer would be the height of folly. Because to get any closer would be to risk getting emotionally involved...

It could happen—she'd be a fool to imagine it couldn't. Simon Devlin's masculine appeal was more potent than any other man's she had ever known. There would be a very real danger of losing not only her heart, but her mind and her will-power as well. For her own emotional survival, she must never let that happen! Because his wants and needs would never match hers. She could well find herself, in her weakened emotional state, agreeing to something she was bound to regret later on. And that would be fatal for both of them.

Best to keep at a safe distance now—while she was still reasonably heartwhole and in command of her mind!

Going back was a lot easier than coming up. Perhaps, because of this, Tanya relaxed and let down her guard— and that was how it happened.

She didn't have any warning. One minute she was picking her way over a clump of rocks that lay in her path, the next she was tumbling down a mossy slope into a gully of ferns, her left arm twisting beneath her as she fell.

She groaned aloud.

Simon leapt after her, seemingly heedless of his own footing, his own safety.

'Tanya, are you all right?'

He dropped to his knees beside her, his great bulk blotting out the sun—and, she dimly noted, flattening a few more ferns in the process. His eyes were dark with concern as his hands moved over her, feeling her all over as tenderly as if she were made of glass.

'Where does it hurt?' he demanded.

She touched her elbow. 'Here... but it's all right. I twisted it, that's all.'

He felt it carefully, bending it, straightening it, pressing here and there. 'You're right. Nothing's broken, thank heavens. But are you sure it feels all right?'

'I'm sure. It's feeling better already.'

His face cleared. 'Here, let me help you up.' He slid his arm beneath her, bringing his face close to hers. She happened just then to glance up at him, and saw with a jolt that he was looking down at *her*.

In the next heart-stopping moment, she had the feeling that she was sinking, drowning in his silvery gaze. Neither moved for a long moment—they might have been frozen like the rocks around them. And then, in a kind of trance, she saw his head coming down, his face blurring over hers as his lips captured hers in a kiss that sent her senses reeling, destroying all her logic, all her self-will, and scattering them to the four winds.

'You're a temptress, do you know that?' he whispered against her lips, and he kissed her again, more ardently, his mouth moving feverishly over hers until her lips parted and seemed to melt. Her whole body was suffused with warmth. Only his mouth on hers existed.

She uttered a soft moan, and he lifted his head and gazed deep into her eyes. As she stared dazedly back, he put a hand to her cheek, his thumb brushing her bruised lips. Her body was on fire, her willpower seemed to have entirely deserted her.

Simon moved his hand down to her throat, then her shoulder. His gaze lowered and at the same time she felt his hand gently moving over the swell of her breast. Dimly, she realised she was straining against him, her nipples tingling, hardening under his touch.

Another low moan escaped her. He was making her feel things she had never felt before. *He*, Simon Devlin, was doing this to her!

Warning bells began ringing in her brain. She mustn't let it go on! This was precisely what she had feared, what mustn't be allowed to happen! It might mean nothing to him, but some inner sense told her that it could be very important to her, that she would be in mortal danger of losing more than her virginity if she succumbed to him now. Some women might be able to play around with a man like Simon Devlin and then calmly walk away, but she... No, she couldn't risk it!

'Simon, I'm sorry!' She wrenched herself away from him. 'I—I don't want this.' She struggled shakily to her feet and began brushing herself down.

He rolled over on to his back among the ferns and glanced up at her with a wry smile. 'You could have fooled me,' he said.

Tanya flushed. 'I must have been stunned for a moment by the fall,' she said, her tone droll as she tried desperately to hide her real emotions from him.

'Well, maybe you were wise to wake up in time,' he murmured as he hoisted his great frame from the ferns. He didn't look hurt or angry—or even disappointed. She couldn't really tell what he was thinking. A mask had come down over his face, and only an enigmatic half-smile remained. Of course, he wouldn't want to get entangled with her any more than she did with him. Thank heavens she had come to her senses in time!

'A momentary aberration,' she said lightly, trying to show him it had meant nothing to her. She started up the slope, and bent over, groaning.

'What's wrong?' He was at her side in a second.

'Nothing.' She gave a giggle—a nervous, high-pitched giggle. 'I feel stiff, that's all. All that climbing! Every muscle aches. I won't be able to walk tomorrow!'

He grinned—a proper grin this time, with genuine amusement in it. 'You've done well,' he commended her, and she felt herself blushing at the unexpected praise. 'I honestly thought you'd never get beyond the first waterfall,' he admitted.

'Well, there, you see—you should never under-
estimate us city girls. Ow—*ouch!*' she gasped as he
grasped her arm and began hauling her up the slope.
'Not so fast! *You sadist!*'

'You'll recover,' he said, still grinning. But there was
a far more amiable note in his voice now than the derisive note she was so used to hearing.

Only then he had to spoil it. 'Come on,' he said when
they were back on the path. 'We'd better get you home.
Back where you belong.'

CHAPTER SIX

THE embezzlement trial ran far longer than originally expected, dragging on day after day. It was a complex case, and the prosecution called many witnesses—most of whom dissolved into confusion and disarray under Simon's penetrating cross-examination.

Tanya, because she was instructing, was in court every day with Simon. Watching him in action at such close quarters, she found herself becoming more impressed each day with his eloquence, his urbanity and poise, his ability to remain unperturbed in any situation. He was very skilful—and a master at putting his opponents off balance.

The jurors—especially the women jurors—hung on his every word. His devastating charm, when he turned it on, was almost irresistible.

Tanya and Simon took their lunch breaks together most days, and they didn't always talk exclusively about the case. They chatted about music and books and current affairs and, to a lesser extent, their families. Tanya learned, with some surprise, that Simon's father had painted most of the oils and watercolours hanging in Simon's country house, and that Simon did a bit of painting himself when he had the time, though his paintings were not for general inspection, he confided to her with a diffidence that she hadn't seen in him before. It made her wonder if that arrogant air of his could be partly an act, a veneer. His years at the bar had, after all, taught him how to act supremely well.

'Do you paint forest landscapes like your father?' she asked, and he nodded.

'My father taught me to love trees,' he said with a brief shrug. 'He knew and loved every tree in those forests, and he passed on his knowledge and his dedication to me...' His voice throbbed with a low passion that caught and held Tanya's attention. She listened, enthralled despite her lack of any real interest in Simon's forest world.

'My father taught me dozens of practical skills,' he went on, making no attempt to hide his pride or his affection. 'Like how to tell if a tree is hollow without felling it; where best to plant and *what* to plant; how to chop and split timber. And he taught me bush cooking and survival skills, and how to enjoy the simple life of a bush camp. I remember sitting in somctimes when my father and the other timber cutters gathered together at the end of the day, often with their wives as well, and argued for hours about politics and events of the time, and just about anything else under the sun.'

Tanya watched his face as he talked, and she began to understand why—from Simon's point of view, at least—he loved the bush so much, and why it kept luring him back. He had obviously had a happy life there, and had been very close—was still close—to both his parents. They sounded intelligent, warm-hearted, family-loving people with wide-ranging interests, and both, apparently, possessed artistic talents which they had passed on to their son. Simon's mother, she recalled, had taught Simon how to play the piano, and from her he must have inherited his love of classical music. And his father had passed on to his son his deep and abiding love of trees and the forest country, and the urge to express that love in painting.

She had to admit—secretly, contritely—that she was surprised. Surprised and impressed. She had so often heard people dismiss Simon Devlin's background with a contemptuous, 'Devlin's had to struggle hard to get where he is today...he was brought up in the bush, you know...son of a timber cutter...' while Simon's mother barely rated a mention, as if she were simply a country housewife with nothing more to offer. So much was left unsaid, so much about them was unknown, unrecognised. They might have been simple, unremarkable folk by sophisticated city standards, they might have been poor in money terms, and their harsh life in the forest country might have been a struggle for them, but their lives had been enriched in ways that few outsiders would ever know about. Or ever care about.

'Why did you come to the city to work, Simon?' she asked curiously. 'If you were so happy in the country, why didn't you become a farmer or a forester or a...or a bush lawyer?'

He looked at her for a long moment, his eyes narrowing imperceptibly. There was something faintly chilling in that shadowed, assessing glance. Surely he didn't think she was having a shot at his background again, that she was insinuating that he didn't belong in the city, while she, with her impeccable background— her moneyed, legal background—did?

'I mean...I'm just a bit surprised that you chose such a—a city-orientated profession,' she amended hastily. 'I guess you must leap at any country briefs that come your way...'

When he made no answer at once, she glanced at him quickly. Oh, dear, surely he didn't think she was *patronising* him now! Nothing was further from her mind!

'I came to the city to make money,' he said coldly, with a dismissive shrug. The curt answer was no doubt intended to forestall any further questions, but instead it gave her something solid to grab hold of, and she ploughed on regardless.

'There must have been easier ways to make money,' she argued.

'Possibly.' Before she could delve any deeper into the whys and wherefores of the choice he'd made, he was adding, with a faintly supercilious lift of one eyebrow, 'I've worked hard and I've been successful. And success has brought its rewards. I have an apartment here in town, and I've built a home that's worth going home to. And I'm building up a business to go with that home.'

Ah, yes . . . his trees. The way he spoke, his tree plantation was more than just a weekend hobby to him. And he made the home he'd built sound like far more than a mere weekend house . . .

'So you do intend to go back to the bush to live,' she said, keeping her tone light, uncaring. Because she *didn't* care. She'd long suspected that the bush would lure him back one day, for good—she'd been hearing whispers to that effect ever since she started practising. That was one of the reasons she knew she must never get involved with him.

Dim chance of that, she thought with a surge of scorn. With every word he uttered, with every look he gave her, he was demonstrating anew how much he rejected everything she stood for, everything she loved the most. There was no doubt about it—they were both poles apart, and they always would be.

She half expected him not to answer her question— after all, what business was it of hers?—and so she was surprised when he did give her an honest answer.

'It's on the cards,' he admitted. 'If I ever marry, I'd like to bring up my kids in the country, at least in their early formative years.'

There was a glint of open mockery in his eyes, as if to disabuse her of any foolish idea that he might have her in mind. Tanya let her own eyes mirror the taunting light in his, to show him how foolish *he* would be to imagine that she might harbour any such foolishness. They were only together now because of this court case. When it was over they would never have to see each other again...

Which didn't prevent her wondering fleetingly what sort of woman Simon Devlin would choose for a wife. Would he choose one of his chic city girlfriends, assuming he could find one who would be willing to give up the fast city life and bury herself in the bush? Or would he choose a placid, down-to-earth country girl who had never known any other life, and so would never hanker after the bright city lights? But would a girl who had lived in the country all her life be stimulating enough *intellectually* for a man like Simon Devlin? With the thought came the swift reminder of Simon's own mother, who had taught him to love music and who had discussed politics and current affairs with the men, and Tanya felt ashamed.

'The bush is a great place to bring up kids,' Simon went on, spearing a prawn with his fork. 'Clean air, clear fresh water, nature at your fingertips... It's a place where you don't get things too easily. You face challenges, take on responsibilities, you learn how to survive in harsh conditions—all the things that help to build initiative and self-confidence. Yes, living in the bush is a great grounding for a kid.'

Tanya looked down at her plate. She had no wish to talk about children. His children. Any children. And she most certainly didn't want to talk about the advantages of living in the bush.

'Tell me about the rest of your family—your brother and sister,' she said, simply to change the subject. 'Do they share your passion for the bush? Your sister married a farmer, I think you said?'

'Yes, Maggie's a real country girl.' His tone was sardonic. 'She never wanted to live anywhere else. Before she married Mike she worked locally, in the bakery. She's a great cook. She could have been a great singer...'

'My, what a talented family!' Tanya couldn't resist a bantering note. 'Painting, music...and now singing too. Why didn't she...?' She trailed off, expecting Simon to snap back that they had been too poor to afford singing lessons, or too poor to send Maggie to the city, let alone overseas, to study.

'She didn't want to leave home,' he said with a brief lift of his shoulders. 'She and Mike were childhood sweethearts...she didn't want to leave him. She was happy to sing at local functions, and occasionally she agreed to sing in some of the bigger country towns. But she never had the ambition or the urge to take it any further.'

'While you did,' said Tanya, her eyes speculative under their fringe of thick lashes.

'Yes, I did,' he said shortly. He didn't say any more, and she didn't press him. But she still felt faintly puzzled that he should have chosen law, of all professions—of all the careers open to him—if his only consideration had been to make money. What else lay behind his decision that he wasn't telling her? What else had he been looking for? Social acceptance? Standing in the community? But neither of those things held water, in Simon Devlin's case. He had never sought social position or personal recognition. Rather, he avoided both like the plague!

Professional recognition, then? The bar was an ego trip for many barristers, thrusting them into the limelight. Or maybe being at the bar gave him a feeling of power? Power over people's lives, over opponents...

Still unsatisfied, she stifled a faint sigh. Simon Devlin was an enigma. But, tempted as she was to probe deeper, to get at the truth, his attitude towards her held her back. She felt she hadn't sufficiently gained his trust, or his respect, to expect him to confide in her to such a degree. And with the differences between them, and the surges of antagonism that still flared between them on occasion, it was unlikely he ever would!

'And your brother?' she asked. He'd been happy enough to talk about his sister. Let him talk about his family, if he didn't want to talk about himself.

'Christopher?' Simon paused, and in that pause Tanya sensed that he didn't particularly want to talk about his brother either. He seemed to be weighing something in his mind. Whether she, an outsider, was worthy of his confidences? she wondered.

'He's living in Adelaide, you said?' she prompted. She knew she should have taken the hint and casually switched to another topic—she could have done it quite easily, since their lunch break was nearly over—but some stubborn impulse urged her to press on. She wanted— and the thought surprised her—to learn more about Simon Devlin. And the key to Simon, she sensed, was his family, his background. She wasn't sure *why* she was so keen to learn more about him, when their time together was likely to be limited. It was just that——

She stole a glance at his face from beneath her sweeping lashes. Below that cool, urbane exterior she sensed that there was a lot more to learn. The little she had discovered already only made the rest more intriguing...

Simon leaned back in his chair. 'Yes, Chris lives in Adelaide. He...had a bit of bad luck over here, and decided to go and look for work in South Australia. He found a job with a builder—the kind of work he'd done before. Chris always wanted to build things, even as a kid. He ended up marrying the builder's daughter Carol. When her father died Chris took over the business. He's doing well. Very well.' Simon lifted his glass and drained the contents. 'Ready to go?'

He hadn't, Tanya noted wryly, confided in her to the extent of revealing what kind of bad luck had driven his brother away from home in the first place. But she guessed it wasn't important now that his brother had made a success of his life. Simon no doubt considered it none of her business anyway.

Later in the week, as they were leaving the courtroom, Simon said casually, 'I've a couple of tickets for Yehudi Menuhin's recital at the Concert Hall tonight. Like to come?'

'I heard he was in town,' she said calmly, matching his own tone with an effort. She didn't feel quite so calm inside. This was the first time Simon had invited her out socially—purely for pleasure. The lunches didn't count—they were business lunches. And her weekend in the bush definitely didn't count, because that had been basically business too. Why was Simon asking *her* and not one of his other women friends? Simply because she was here, on the spot?

'If you're already going...' Simon said indifferently.

'No, I'm not.' She enjoyed going to concerts, but she had been so wrapped up in the trial this week that she hadn't done anything about arranging to go to this one, and none of her friends had suggested going. Ellie, for one, preferred jazz concerts. 'I'd love to,' she said. He's only asking me because he knows I play the violin, she concluded. Anyone with a love of the violin, of good music, would jump at the chance to go and hear Menuhin, who, she'd heard, still played sublimely, even though he was over seventy now. Simon was just being thoughtful... it was no big deal.

But in a way it *was* a big deal, because it revealed another aspect of Simon Devlin's character. He was thoughtful. He noticed things, remembered things. Most men she knew would have forgotten that throwaway remark of hers about having learned to play the violin.

'You don't need to go home and change, do you?' Simon's tone was laconic.

Tanya translated that as *I'd rather you didn't*. She looked down at her pleated skirt and ruffled white blouse, and guessed it would do at a pinch. But she felt slightly irritated. He was imposing his will on her again! Surely she had time to pop home to her flat and freshen up and change before the concert? It wouldn't start until eight.

'I thought we might have a bite of dinner together before the concert,' he said before she could answer, or get too steamed up. 'There's a Chinese restaurant overlooking the river, just a hop away from the Concert Hall. They're putting on a special pre-concert meal, starting early. I've booked a table.'

He had booked a table, before he'd even asked her! She smiled faintly at her reaction. Why get uptight about it? No doubt he would still have eaten there whether she had joined him or not. Was there anything so wrong in making plans in advance?

It's just his way, she concluded as she nodded acceptance. He's so used to running his own life, to making decisions, to issuing orders. Surely it was better to be decisive than to shilly-shally around like some of the men she knew, who were forever deferring to her, so over-anxious to please that they were content to let her call all the shots. She had hardly realised until now just how tiresome that could be.

She flashed a sudden smile, drawing an answering, if somewhat quizzical, smile from Simon. Let Simon Devlin have his head, she thought with a new-found equanimity. She would go along with him for just as long as his decisions coincided with her own. The day they didn't, she would let him know in no uncertain terms!

'Where have you been?' asked Ellie as she walked in. 'Not working again?'

Tanya shook her head. Because she had been occupied in court each day this week, she had worked back a couple of nights to catch up on her other work. 'I went to Yehudi Menuhin's recital,' she said carelessly, and headed for the kitchen, hoping Ellie wouldn't ask with whom.

She might have known it was a futile hope. Ellie followed her. 'Oh? That was nice. Who did you go with? Your mother?'

'Simon Devlin had a couple of tickets. Ellie, don't read anything into it,' she begged as Ellie's brown eyes lit up. 'How was *your* evening?'

'Boring. I stayed home and watched a pathetic film on TV. Tan, tell me about your night. What *happened*?'

'Nothing happened. Nothing to tell.' Tanya's soft hair fell across her face as she poured herself a cup of coffee. 'Simon just happened to have a spare ticket and I was around, so he asked me. I'd mentioned to him once that I'd learned to play the violin.'

'And he remembered.' Ellie raised her eyebrows. 'Considerate of him.'

Tanya ignored that, even though she'd had much the same thought. 'The recital was wonderful,' she said, handing Ellie a cup of coffee. 'Menuhin still has the old magic. He played a Beethoven sonata...and a Bach suite...and a Mozart——'

'Uh-huh. Where did you eat?' Ellie wasn't interested in the concert.

'We had a quick Chinese meal before the recital.' No need to dwell on the camaraderie that had grown between them during that rushed meal, the laughter that she and Simon had shared as they fumbled with their chopsticks, as they bit into the searingly hot chillies in their sweet-and-sour chicken, and as they gulped down the cooling house wine, and later as they had run through the rain to the Concert Hall. The warmth, the camaraderie, had stayed with them during the recital, as they listened, enraptured, to the maestro weaving his spell over the entranced audience.

She had glimpsed Nick Manning-Smith in the concert hall, a few rows in front of them. He had had a girl with him, and his head was close to hers. Strangely, Tanya had felt no reaction, not the slightest twinge of jealousy, of regret. She had done the right thing in breaking off with Nick. She had never been able to respond to him the way he would have liked. Idly, she now found herself wondering why. He was good-looking, charming, ambitious, and her parents had been all in favour of a match between them. But for some reason she had backed away the moment Nick had started to get serious. His possessive attitude had irritated her, turned her off. At the time she had thought it was because of her career, because she hadn't wanted to jeopardise that. Nick would have demanded that she give it up if she married him. But she knew now that the chemistry just hadn't been right.

Either that, or she was frigid! And remembering, with a faint flush, the way Simon Devlin's kisses, his touch, could turn her body to fire, even without any special feeling or regard between them, she couldn't in all honesty believe that she was.

After the concert, Simon had driven her home, ignoring her protests that she could quite easily catch a tram. In the confines of his car, she had suddenly felt startlingly aware of his physical presence, his proximity, and the fact that they were now quite alone. In the concert hall, even though they had been sitting even closer together, even though more than once she had felt his arm brushing against hers, she had been far less aware of him there—because there had been other people around them, she supposed. In the confines of his car it was different, and she had wondered nervously, at the time, if Simon was aware of the way his presence was affecting her, of the tension she was feeling, of the electricity, like a palpable force, that she could feel flowing between them. She sincerely hoped not. How he'd laugh, how he'd crow, if he thought that she was as susceptible as the other women in his life! The other women who came and went...

Because they did come and go, she reflected, gripping her coffee-cup tightly and trying not to think of the way she had almost stumbled from Simon's car when he had pulled up outside her flat. He was rarely seen with the same woman more than once. When was he going to find a woman he wouldn't want to let go of so easily? Where would he find this perfect creature he was looking for—a woman who would be willing to give up everything to follow him into the wilds?

Take care, Tanya Barrington, she cautioned, recalling the almost panicky way she had thanked him and fled inside. You're in danger of falling under his all-too-potent spell. Can't you see that it's only because he's here in the city now, in *your* world, that you're starting to find him desirable? But he won't *stay* here...he's a bushman at heart, and he'll always be a bushman. And a bush*woman* is something you will never be! Or ever *want* to be.

'You've got it bad,' Ellie said knowingly, her voice breaking in on Tanya's thoughts and bringing a telltale flush to her cheeks.

'Don't be silly,' Tanya said sharply, setting down her empty cup. 'I'm going to bed. Goodnight!'

The end of the week came and the trial was still going. As the court was adjourned for the weekend, Simon took his leave of Tanya on the steps outside the building.

'See you Monday,' he said, looking down at her. He was still wearing his wig and gown, and he towered over her, the slanting rays of the dying sun behind his back, throwing his imposing frame into sharp relief and rimming his outline with shimmering gold. She had the strangest, most ridiculous feeling, the insane desire to slip inside that voluminous gown of his and press her head against his strong, hard chest. She dismissed the feeling in a trice—she was hardly the dependent, submissive type! She must be tired, that was all, after her long week in court.

'You're off to the bush for the weekend?' she asked him lightly, and was conscious of a faint pang when he nodded. Had she honestly believed that he might stay in town, simply because they had had a few companionable moments during the week? She devoutly hoped that he hadn't noticed any change in her face, any flicker of disappointment. She didn't want him getting the idea that she was interested in him. Because really nothing had changed. And she would do well to keep that in mind.

'What plans do *you* have?' he was asking.

Did he really want to know? she wondered wistfully. 'There's a party tomorrow night,' she said, trying to look and sound enthusiastic. 'Somebody's birthday.' She shrugged. 'Nothing much else. The market in the morning. Maybe tennis on Sunday.'

'Talking of tennis,' Simon said idly, 'I've some workmen coming in tomorrow to start levelling an area for a tennis court.'

Tanya took a careful breath. 'That'll be nice,' she said, and hoped her words didn't sound as stilted to him as they did to her own ears. So he was building a tennis court now... Just one more way of making his bush property into a home... Just one more way of letting her know that he wouldn't be staying in the city indefinitely...

Thanks for the warning, Simon. But I don't need it. I already know.

'Well, enjoy yourself,' said Simon, and she watched him stride away, unaware if he had even heard her lighthearted, 'You too.'

*   *   *

The party was in full swing, but Tanya kept glancing at her watch, wishing it were later so that she could make her escape. She had never known an evening, a party, to drag so. She couldn't quite work out why. They were a bright enough crowd, and she knew just about everybody there. All the ingredients to make a successful party were there... laughter, food, drink, lively stereo music, a room full of friends. If the stories and jokes were mostly ones she'd already heard—well, so what? She'd laughed at them before, and they were still amusing. Only tonight she found it an effort even to raise a smile.

Was she bored? Or was she simply tired? It must be one or the other. Maybe it was because Ellie wasn't there. Ellie and her latest beau had gone fishing for the weekend. Ellie, *fishing*! That did bring a smile. Ellie must be really keen on this one...

'May I share the joke?' asked a voice, and Tanya turned to meet a pair of admiring blue eyes above a broadly smiling mouth.

'Oh...James. Hi. I was just...well, never mind.' James Hendry was one of the up-and-coming young stockbrokers about town, the son of a close friend of her father's. A well-mannered, well-bred young bachelor-who-was-going-places. All of which made him highly eligible... as her father had hinted more than once since her break-up from Nick. James, like Nick, was one of the polished-to-the-eyeballs clones that Ellie had recently teased her about. He was not only a clone, but also, in Tanya's opinion, a bore. Given half a chance, he would talk money, and stocks and shares, all night.

'I had a function at the Club before I came here,' James said in his rather pompous way. Tanya was sorely tempted to respond with an impish, 'Oh? Which football club is that?' but she refrained, aware that he lacked a sense of humour, and knowing full well that in James's restricted world there was only one club, the Melbourne Club. According to her father, James was one of the youngest members ever to be admitted.

'I was just about to leave,' she said swiftly, knowing that if she stayed she would be stuck with him for the rest of the evening. She silently thanked her lucky stars that she had brought her own car. At least he wouldn't be able to insist on driving her home.

'Oh, not already.' James's brilliant smile faded. 'I've only just arrived. Let me drive you home,' he said in the next breath.

'Good of you, James, but I have my own car. And as you say, you've only just arrived. Stay and enjoy the party. It's just starting to swing.'

Just starting to take a distinct nosedive, Tanya amended under her breath as she slipped away. James had never got under her skin quite so irritatingly before. Why tonight? She had always known what he was like, and yet she had always been willing enough to put up with him in the past, had always found him pleasant enough company before. Why could she barely tolerate him tonight?

He wants to move in on me, now that I'm no longer going out with Nick...that's why he's getting on my nerves, she concluded. And I don't want him hassling me. I don't want *him*, full stop. It's as simple as that.

She pulled a face as she thrust her key into the ignition. If there was any other possible reason for her discontent this evening, for the restlessness, the irritability, the boredom that was assailing her, she certainly wasn't going to delve into the possible reasons now. She was far too worn out, physically and mentally!

Tomorrow, she would work off any remaining list-lessness on the tennis court.

CHAPTER SEVEN

WHEN she saw Simon Devlin's tall, imposing figure in the court room on Monday morning, Tanya's heart did a slow roll and then settled into a skittering, thudding rhythm. She felt blood rushing to her face, bringing a rosy flush to her cheeks, an over-brightness to her eyes, the start of a smile to her lips.

And Simon chose that very moment to turn around and face her.

His eyes met hers across the room, and for what seemed an endless moment she felt her gaze locked to his. She was aware of a stifling sensation, as if she were wearing a collar that was far too tight, or was in a room that was too warm. Only today she was wearing a dress with no constricting collar, and the chill of early morning still hung over the courtroom. What was Simon Devlin doing to her? My goodness, she thought, if he should notice!

She dropped her gaze first, desperately trying to regain her equilibrium, aware of how ridiculous she was being. Reacting like this to the sight of Simon Devlin! Almost suffocating, merely because he was looking at her! He was only acknowledging her presence, merely saying a silent 'hello'... He could hardly shout out 'hello' across the courtroom. It wouldn't be seemly.

It came as a shock to realise that Simon could affect her this way. A man she had no intention of ever getting involved with. A man whose way of life would never coincide with hers. A man, moreover, who would never want her anyway—except possibly as a temporary diversion, to dominate, possess, and then carelessly discard. Simon would never seriously involve himself with the pampered daughter of Mr Justice Barrington—a dyed-in-the-wool city girl, who hated the bush.

With that in mind, she managed to face him with at least an outward calm.

'You had lovely weather for your weekend,' she said. It was an effort to speak naturally, but she managed it—just.

'So did you.' His eyes swept over her face, and she had to steel herself not to react. 'Warm, clear, and not too hot.' He winked at her. 'No rain to bring out the spiders, no heat to bring out the snakes...'

'I knew you'd never let me live any of that down.' It was easier than she had expected to talk about it—to laugh about it, even if the laugh was on her. 'Aren't you forgetting the possums?'

'Oh, I'm not forgetting anything,' he said, a silvery glint in his eye, and this time Tanya flushed. That aspect of their weekend together she wasn't so ready to laugh about. Least of all right now, when her emotions were so——

But she mustn't think about any of that. There was no point, no future in it.

'How is your tennis court coming along?' she asked with a sprightliness she was sure he saw through, because his eyes were openly laughing at her now. Mocking her. Oh, yes, he remembered all right. He remembered everything.

'There's a long way to go yet. How was your tennis game yesterday?'

'It was all right. Fine,' she amended, trying to sound enthusiastic. She had enjoyed the game, but she had still felt strangely listless all day, as if something was lacking, or not quite right. She had finally admitted to herself late last night, as she lay tossing restlessly in her bed, that what she had been missing over the weekend was Simon Devlin's company! A jolting realisation. Once she had recognised the problem—because it *was* a problem, a problem with only one resolution—it had been easier. She had been able to put up all the old arguments about their differences, about how a relationship between them would never work out, even if Simon wanted it too, about how disastrous it would be to allow her emotions sweep her into something that could lead precisely nowhere.

She would get over these feelings when she saw him again, she had ended up convincing herself. Over the weekend, for some foolish reason, she had built up a romantic, unreal, exaggerated picture of him in her mind, simply because she was tired, and a bit bored, and he wasn't around to bring her back to earth. Once she saw him again, once they were working side by side in court, where she would be forced to face up to the harsh realities of their situation and the futility of getting involved, she would quickly come back to earth and regain her senses. And by the time the trial ended, she would, she fervently hoped, have him thoroughly out of her system.

She even half hoped that he would flaunt one of his most stunning-looking women friends under her nose at some time during the trial. If anything was going to dampen her ardour, that should do it quicker than anything!

Only there had been no instant cure when she saw him again, no lessening of her unwise, irrational yearning for him. Her reaction just now, to the mere sight of him in the courtroom, had startled and dismayed her. But all was not lost. She was still in possession of her mind—she could still *think* . . . and her rational side told her that she had to kill what she felt there and then, no matter how much her emotions might be urging her otherwise.

When lunchtime came, she heard herself babbling, 'I have to go back to the office—I have some calls to make. I—I'll be back after lunch,' and she fled, avoiding Simon's eyes.

And when the court was adjourned for the day, she didn't give him a chance to suggest dinner. 'I must fly. I have a lot of work to catch up on. I'll be working back at the office tonight . . . in fact, every night this week.'

She cast a wary look up at him. Could he see through her? There was a hint of derision in his eyes. Did he guess that she was running away from him? Did he guess that she was trying to keep at a safe distance? Worse, did he guess how she was beginning to feel about him? How it must be amusing him, when his own emotions were not even touched!

He didn't attempt to dissuade her, didn't suggest dinner or anything else, either that night or the next, and Tanya spent two miserable if busily occupied evenings at her office desk, munching sandwiches as she worked, trying to convince herself that she was relieved he wasn't making things difficult for her by trying to tempt her away from her work—and yet disappointed, deep down, when he didn't.

Obviously Simon didn't care about her at all, didn't *want* her company, and she'd be a proper little fool if she let it bother her. She ought to be grateful to him for making it easier for her.

Another day dragged by in court, and she had to admit to herself that it wasn't working—she was becoming more conscious of Simon with each minute that ticked by. She tried to tell herself that she was sorry he hadn't flaunted any of his women friends during the week, but she knew in her heart that she was glad, and that she would have felt like clawing their eyes out if he had.

The thought gave her a jolt. What in the world was happening to her? She'd never felt like this about any man before in her life. She'd never felt jealous before in her life. She had better pull herself together before she became totally obsessed.

On her third night back at the office, another wet miserable night—it had rained all week—she was startled by a rap on the door. Nobody but Ellie knew she was here, and Ellie had gone to a film tonight. Tanya bit her lip. Nobody else but——

She felt herself go hot and cold all over, felt her throat constrict. For a moment she couldn't move, couldn't even call out.

And then the door opened and Simon Devlin strode in.

'Ah, so you *are* still here!' He ambled across the room, his hands thrust deep in the pockets of his navy sports jacket. 'I had to come and see for myself, Tanya Barrington actually working late at the office every night!'

'You're checking up on me!' She seized on anger to hide the other emotions she felt. 'What did you think I was doing—kicking up my heels, having a night out on the town?'

'I'm not sure what I thought.' Quite an admission for Simon Devlin—being uncertain about anything! 'I only know you've been looking mighty peaky the past couple of days, and I wanted to find out why. It's not like you.'

'Working late makes you pale and peaky...I'm a bit behind, that's all. I told you I had work to catch up on.'

'So you did. And so you are...catching up on it.' There was surprise, a new respect in his eyes.

She reacted indignantly, wanting to hide the other feelings his presence here was arousing.

'You still think I'm just a good-time girl, don't you? You think the law is just a game, a pastime to me. You think I'm just playing at it—that others are doing the real work and just kidding me along, bolstering me up...'

Simon eyed her steadily for a long moment. 'I did once think along those lines,' he admitted honestly. 'But you've shown me that you do know your job...that you do it thoroughly and well and that you care about it. I owe you an apology.'

'Well, thank you.' Tanya tried to sound gracious as she felt her anger ebbing away. An apology from the great Simon Devlin wasn't to be sneezed at.

So he respected her now, did he? He respected her *work* at least, respected her dedication to the legal profession. But when was he going to respect her as a *person* as well? As a private individual, a *woman*? When was he going to realise that she had changed, that she was no longer the rather flighty, fast-living city socialite she had been when they first met—a girl who, outside working hours, thought only of having a good time and flitting from one polished clone to the next? She was no longer that girl. None of those things seemed to mean anything to her any more.

But how could she explain any of that to Simon without telling him *why* they meant nothing, without admitting that she——

That she what? That she was attracted to him? Well, that she would never admit to! Because it was a futile attraction. They both wanted different things out of life, both wanted to live in different worlds. Simon wanted to live permanently in his beloved bush world, a world she would never fit into, would never *want* to fit into. She was a city girl and always would be. And Simon was straining at the leash to leave town for good.

'I'd better go home,' she said soberly. 'It's late, and I'm desperately tired.'

'I'll drive you,' he said, and there was a tenderness in his voice that she had never heard before. She saw something in his eyes as well, an expression that wasn't so easy to interpret—a whole tangle of emotions that she couldn't begin to unravel. And mustn't, for her own peace of mind, even try to.

The next morning the long trial ended and the jury retired to consider its verdict. They were out for most of the day. Simon was hopeful, but by no means over-confident. He had vigorously challenged the evidence, and the witnesses, and his meticulous defence had almost certainly left sufficient questions and doubts in the jurors' minds to find in favour of their client. But one never knew.

Tanya excused herself and slipped back to her office while she was waiting for the result, Simon making no attempt to stop her. She hadn't been able to meet his eye all morning, though she had hung on his every word during his brilliant summing up, and had tried to transmit to him by telepathy rather than direct eye contact her moral support and encouragement.

As if he needed any encouragement from her! She might be his briefing solicitor, but until recently he had seen her as a raw young socialite-lawyer who couldn't prepare her own briefs without help! She shouldn't get too carried away with what he had said about her last night. Not if she had any sense.

She was recalled to the courtroom late in the afternoon, arriving back just as the jury were filing in.

A wave of surprised relief swept over the crowded courtroom when the jury brought in a 'Not guilty' verdict. The defendant, a quiet, reserved man, had touched the sympathy of everyone, court and jurors alike. It was a great victory for Simon.

'Congratulations.' Tanya leaned towards him with a smile. 'Another triumph for Simon Devlin...' She had automatically thrust out her hand, and now she realised that his own had closed over hers, and he still hadn't let it go.

Then others crowded around, and after a moment Simon seemed to realise that he was still holding her hand and released it. But for some time afterwards her hand still tingled from his touch, and she was acutely aware of the impression his warm flesh had left on hers.

She had to go to Simon's chambers afterwards to pick up the relevant papers and documents for costing. As she was turning to leave, wondering bleakly if she would ever see him again, Simon looked up from his desk and said, 'Like to go out and celebrate this evening?' Though his voice was low and compelling, his grey eyes, shadowed by his half-closed lids, were unreadable.

Tanya took a deep breath. No need to get excited. No need to read anything into it. Naturally he'd want to celebrate, to unwind a bit. It had been a long trial. But——

'It's Friday,' she said, thinking he must have forgotten.

'So? You have some objection to celebrating on a Friday?' His lip quirked. 'Or do you have something better to do?'

'It's not that,' she said, and wondered afterwards why she hadn't simply seized the excuse he was offering, pleaded another engagement, and kept at a safe distance. 'You always go bush at weekends,' she said.

'I'll drive up in the morning. I'll still have plenty of time up there. It's a long weekend,' he reminded her.

She had almost forgotten the holiday on Monday. Normally she would have planned to go away somewhere for the long weekend, but this time she hadn't bothered. Ellie was going to Portsea with some of their usual crowd, but when Tanya heard that James Hendry was going too she had bowed out. She couldn't face the thought of fighting him off for a whole weekend.

'How are you planning to celebrate?' she asked Simon cautiously. If she'd gone away with Ellie, she wouldn't have been home tonight to celebrate with Simon. Would that have been a good or a bad thing? she found herself wondering, her heart giving a tiny flutter.

'With a long, lingering dinner by candlelight...' At the startled flare in her eyes, he added easily, 'After the glare and blare of the past few days, I'd say bright lights and loud music were definitely out, wouldn't you? A quiet, relaxed evening, now... doesn't that sound more enticing?'

Tanya nodded slowly. 'Where did you have in mind?' As it was Friday night, most of the more popular city restaurants would be crowded and noisy—hardly the atmosphere Simon had in mind—and, as far as she knew, Simon wasn't in the habit of frequenting the more exclusive, sedate establishments, where quiet, lingering dinners by candlelight were regular nightly fare.

Her vague misgivings were realised when he answered coolly, 'How about my flat? It's peaceful and comfortable there, and we can listen to the music *we* want to hear, and not what's foisted on to us.'

'But you'd have to cook your own dinner,' she protested, aware of a prickling sensation popping out all over her skin. With her eyes she told him, If you think I'm going to be one of your convenient here-today-gone-tomorrow women, Simon Devlin, you're very much mistaken!

'I like to cook,' he said, looking up from his desk with amusement in his eyes. In her heightened state of tension, his eyes held a distinctly Machiavellian gleam. This is a game to him, she thought, breathing hard. A game he's often played... Well, Simon, my friend, it's one I'm not joining in!

She wouldn't dare!

'I know of a place that's quiet... and you wouldn't have to do a thing,' she said in desperation. 'I'm sure I could get a booking there at short notice...'

'I'm sure you could,' drawled Simon, his tone clearly saying, *with your name and influence*...

This so incensed her, partly because there was a grain of truth in what he was implying and partly because he could never seem to resist having a shot at her privileged family background, that she stubbornly dug in her heels.

'I'll go and try now... what's the time?' She glanced at her watch, and as she did so the pile of papers she was juggling under her arm spilt on to the floor. 'Damn!' She dropped the briefcase she had been gripping in her other hand and knelt down to gather them up again. Hell, she was never as clumsy as this! What was happening to her?

'If you were a gentleman, you'd help me with these papers,' she snapped as she tottered to her feet.

Simon, all this while, had remained at his desk, sitting back and watching her with a maddening half-smile on his lips. He had made no attempt to jump up and help her pick them up. Any other man she knew would have rushed to her aid.

'You were managing all right without me,' he murmured, and she had the feeling that his words held a double meaning. He seemed to be hinting that since she was taking charge of the evening, dictating where they should go, she was perfectly capable of taking charge of a few wayward papers as well!

She stood for a moment, glowering at him. Plainly, Simon Devlin wasn't accustomed to having a woman dictate to him and make the decisions. The trouble with Simon, she decided in exasperation, was that he had had only himself to consider for so long that he had never bothered to consider what anybody else might want! Let alone a woman. *How about my flat?* he'd suggested, expecting her to jump at the offer, as no doubt a string of other women had fallen over themselves to do—and would undoubtedly go on doing in the future! Well, I'm not one of your fawning, submissive, easy-come-easy-go women, Simon Devlin, Tanya thought crossly, and if I ever step foot in your flat, it won't be for the reason *you* have in mind!

'Look...' Simon rose from his desk and moved towards her, his hands half raised now—for what purpose she was unsure, but just in case he had any intention of placing them on her shoulders, or anywhere else, she took a wary step backwards. As she did so, he paused. Had he seen the wariness, the near-panic in her eyes?

'Look,' he said again, 'I think you've got the wrong idea. I was only offering dinner and a bit of music...nothing else, I assure you. A relaxing evening.

Just that.' The corner of his lip tilted slightly. 'If you come to my flat I promise I'll keep the bedroom door firmly shut—locked, if you like. I know how the sight of a bed can alarm you.'

Her cheeks flamed. It hadn't been the sight of his bed that time that had alarmed her. It had been the sight of the man in it...the feel of his arms...the touch of——

'Just dinner...and a bit of music,' she repeated, nodding mindlessly as she tried to regain her old coolness, the self-possession that had once been second nature to her—until Simon Devlin had come along and shattered it. How do I know I can trust you? was what she was really saying. How do I know I can trust myself? was what she meant.

'I assure you I don't seduce every woman I bring home to my flat.' His tone was whimsical. 'I'm not the Casanova you seem to think I am. And I have never forced myself on a woman yet. I've never needed to,' he added drily, and when she met his eye, she saw that the grey had turned to glinting silver.

Is that a snide little reminder of the night I came to his bedroom? she wondered suspiciously. Or is he thinking of the next afternoon, when I fell down the slope and he—and I——

She tilted her chin defiantly. Well, he ought to be getting the message now...that she didn't want to get into anything heavy with him. Not that Simon Devlin would see a brief affair, a casual romp, as anything 'heavy'. It wouldn't mean a thing to him—he would make sure he didn't let his feelings get involved. But Tanya wasn't so sure that she could keep her own feelings out of it. And she wasn't prepared to take the risk. Because any deep, lasting relationship between them was impossible, out of the question. Which he must know as well as she.

'Here,' he said, his hand reaching for the papers she was clutching. Clutching as if for dear life! 'Let me help you to your car.'

They were in his arms before she could protest. Shrugging, she gave in. It would be petty to refuse, just as it would be petty to insist on seeking out a safe, quiet restaurant for dinner, when he was offering her comfortable dining, pleasant music, and uninterrupted conversation at his own flat. She would accept his invitation... and if he tried anything, if he betrayed the trust she was showing in him by changing her mind, then she would refuse to see him again. Ever.

Simple as that.

On the dot of eight o'clock the doorbell rang. Simon had insisted on picking her up at her flat. 'We'll be drinking champagne and wine,' he had cautioned earlier, 'and I don't want you driving home over the legal limit. Relax... I won't be driving you home either. I'll call you a cab.'

It wasn't the drive home that she was worried about—it was the thought of the champagne and the wine—and the raffish intentions Simon Devlin might be harbouring. She still didn't know whether she could trust him to keep his word. A man with a reputation as a womaniser—despite his denials!

Simon's flat was functional, neat, and comfortable, the décor neutral and relaxing, the atmosphere unthreatening. There was a small modern kitchen, a cosy living-dining-room, and two bedrooms—Tanya took Simon's word for that, declining an inspection—one of which he told her, he used as a study. She didn't feel

game enough, sure enough of herself, or of him, to enquire, even facetiously, what he used the other bedroom
for—other than sleeping. She might have risked it with
any other man but Simon Devlin, but with Simon she
was finding that her old breezy self-confidence was distinctly shaky lately.

Feeling the way she did about him—and she couldn't
deny that she did, against all reason, all logic, feel something—being alone like this with Simon Devlin was rather
like sitting on a keg of unexploded gunpowder. And yet,
in other ways, the evening turned out to be one of the
most relaxed, most enjoyable evenings of her life.

Simon conjured up a superb meal at short notice, a
delicious concoction of stir-fried beef and noodles with
a crisp green salad, topping the dinner off with fresh
ripe strawberries and orange segments marinated in
Cointreau. A quiet dinner by candlelight, as promised.
Any pauses in the conversation, and there were surprisingly few, were pleasantly filled by Mozart, Chopin,
and the glorious voice of Cleo Laine—Simon's choice
of the latter delighting Tanya because it showed that
Simon had wide tastes in music, and that here again their
tastes coincided.

Simon was a brilliant conversationalist, his lively mind
coming up with a range of topics to debate and discuss.
He was charming, agreeable and considerate, and she
quickly found herself relaxing. It was only when she was
gathering up her bag and jacket in readiness for the cab
he had dutifully summoned for her that she realised he
hadn't made a single pass at her all evening—and hadn't
made a single gibe either about her background or her
pleasure-loving city lifestyle. Was he at last beginning to
see her as the girl she really was, rather than the playgirl

she had been happy enough in the past to let him—as she had let other men—think she was?

Why then—*why*?—did she have to go and spoil it? Better to have cut off her tongue than ask what she did, and unthinkingly trigger off their only brush of the evening. As she was thanking him, she asked him teasingly, 'Slaving away on your tree plantation this weekend, Simon?'

Perhaps it was the effect of the wine she had consumed, or perhaps it was simply the euphoric aftermath of the unexpectedly pleasant evening, but she failed to notice immediately the hardening of his eyes, failed to be warned by his tone, as he answered, so softly that she almost missed the words, 'If you want to call it that.' Imprudently, she followed her first question with another, in the same teasing vein.

'Don't you ever take a weekend off to relax?'

In the silence—the agonising silence—that followed, she glanced up into his face, and met the diamond-hard glitter in his eyes. That was when she first sensed that something was wrong, and realised that she had foolishly exposed herself to one of his sharp put-downs. When it came, she winced, even though his tone was remote rather than sharp.

'Hard work can be relaxing to some people...if they're used to it.'

Her eyes wavered under his. 'Are you implying that I'm not?' she asked hoarsely, cursing herself for opening her mouth in the first place. Just when she had been so sure that he was beginning to see her in a new, more praiseworthy light!

He shrugged. 'Well...can you honestly say that you are?'

Tanya drew in a deep breath. She wanted to let it go, but she couldn't. Better, perhaps, to have it out now. 'Why don't you tell me?' she invited resignedly.

He reached out and ran a finger down her arm, as if to soften the words that followed. 'You've never had to work hard for anything,' he spelt out, his words hard but his tone gentle. 'Everything has come easily to you. You've had your whole life virtually presented to you on a platter.'

'Nobody passed my exams for me,' she shot back, her eyes indignant, hiding her hurt.

'True, but your law course was made easy for you.' His hand slid away, and at his withdrawal she was conscious of a distinct pang, a sense of loss. 'Would you know what it's like to have to work your way through university to pay the rent? To have to share a house with four other students? To drag yourself home after working late into the night at a second job, knowing you had to finish an assignment before you could go to bed? And you had other advantages—you were lucky enough to have lawyers in your family to advise you and help you and make useful introductions and create openings for you.'

Her teeth tugged at her lip. She couldn't deny it. It was all true. She hadn't had to struggle through life the way he had. And having lawyers in her family had had its advantages, there was no doubt about it. But having a legal background was nothing to be ashamed of. Was Simon trying to make her feel guilty?

She rallied, her eyes sparking, the blue splintering into different shades of violet and amethyst. 'You're throwing my advantages in my face. You have a chip on your shoulder because my road was easier than yours——'

She heard his sharp intake of breath. 'You're missing my point,' he rasped. 'I'm not feeling sorry for myself because you had advantages I didn't. I'm proud, as a matter of fact, of what I've had to do. Sure, it wasn't easy, but I've never been afraid of hard work. The bush toughens you, builds your self-confidence, prepares you for the challenges in life. The point I was trying to make is that you, my lovely Tanya, have never had to battle for anything, you've never been up against any truly formidable obstacles, you've never really been *tested*. How hard would you fight, I wonder, if you were?'

She met his gaze. 'I was petrified the first time I went hang-gliding,' she said evenly. 'If I'd wanted to take the easy way out, I'd have stayed on *terra firma.*'

He made an impatient gesture. 'Some would call that recklessness...bravado...even showing off. Hardly facing one of life's real challenges. It was your own choice to do it. It wasn't something you had to do in order to live, to survive...'

She sighed in exasperation. 'Are you saying I haven't any real backbone?'

'I'm saying you've never had to fight hard for anything, to prove whether you have or not. You might very well surprise me one day.'

'So it would be a surprise, would it, if I proved I had a bit of real spunk?' Her tone was sarcastic, but inside she felt bruised, disappointed. After working so closely together in these past days, after seeing each other out of working hours and even after toiling up that mountain with him, Simon still had the same low opinion of her. 'I fight hard for each and every one of my clients,' she growled, thrusting out her chin. 'I'm sorry if I don't come up to your high standards.'

'I wasn't referring to your *ability*, Tanya... I have nothing but admiration for the way you conduct yourself in your practice.'

Well, she thought drily, a compliment at last, from his own lips! It was so unexpected that she didn't know quite how to deal with it. Attack, she decided, was the best way. 'I sense there's a "but" coming,' she said, eyeing him suspiciously.

She felt his hand on her shoulder, and his touch sent a quiver rippling through her. She hoped he wasn't aware of it. 'I'm not saying you lack ability, or spunk, or spirit. I'm merely saying you've never had to face any serious challenges or setbacks in your life... you've never had to fight tooth and nail for anything. I was simply pondering how you would meet the test, that's all.'

And what he was *implying* was that he didn't expect her to come through the test... because her pampered existence had made her so soft, so self-complacent, so indolent, that she wouldn't have the guts to fight to the finish!

'You look very fierce,' he murmured, his lips easing into a smile that tugged at her heart. 'Yes, I believe you may well surprise me one day...' His hand moved up to stroke her hair, his fingers gliding over the soft strands, making her shiver. 'Your hair always looks so soft and bright. And it feels even softer than it looks...'

It was just as well, perhaps, that her cab arrived at that moment.

CHAPTER EIGHT

THE telephone shrilled in her ear, waking her. It was her mother, asking her about the trial, and when she was going to have time to come to dinner.

'What about tonight?' asked Tanya. She felt a bit guilty about not seeing her parents for a while, though she'd kept in contact by phone.

'Tonight? Saturday? But you always go out on a Saturday night, darling! In fact, I'm surprised you haven't gone away for the weekend.'

'I felt like staying home for a change. Are you going to be home tonight?' Her parents seldom had a free Saturday evening themselves.

'We're having some friends over for dinner. But you're welcome to come too, of course.'

Tanya blew out her breath. 'That doesn't sound like my idea of a quiet night. Could I come for lunch instead?'

'Are you all right, dear?' her mother asked sharply. 'You don't sound like yourself. What is it?'

'I'm just a bit tired, that's all. It was a long trial...and I had a late night last night.'

That brought the inevitable question. 'With anyone special?' Her mother had been disappointed when she'd broken off with Nick Manning-Smith. She, like Tanya's father, had been trying to steer her in James Hendry's direction ever since.

'No, no one special. Simon and I had dinner together to celebrate the end of the trial, that's all.'

'Simon? You mean Simon Devlin? You're seeing him *socially* now?'

'I'm not *seeing* him in the way you mean, Mother. He just wanted to thank me for my help during the trial...' Something prompted her to add, 'Why? Would you have any objection if I did see more of him?'

'Not...not really.' Her mother was too shrewd a woman to openly condemn her daughter's choice of men friends. Her father, on the other hand, would have come right out and made his views patently plain. 'I'm just a bit surprised, that's all,' her mother admitted. 'After that awful weekend you said you had...' Tanya had given her mother a brief run-down on her weekend at Simon's, emphasising the more disagreeable aspects—the spiders, the snakes, her aching muscles after climbing in the Baw Baws '...I didn't expect you to want to see him again.'

'Well, I had to, didn't I? We were working together on this case. I'll probably never see him again—socially, that is.' Why did she feel an aching emptiness at the prospect? 'He's nicer than I thought,' she heard herself confessing pensively. 'Once you get to know him he's...he's quite different from the rough, hard-nosed autocrat I thought he was to begin with.' Listen to her! Singing the praises of Simon Devlin, of all men! Her mother *would* be getting ideas if she didn't shut up. 'How's Daddy?' she asked quickly.

'He's right here. Like a word?'

Tanya's heart dipped. Had her father been listening to the conversation? 'Oh—er——'

'What's this about you seeing that young upstart Devlin?'

She drew in a deep breath. 'Upstart, Daddy? That's no way to talk about one of your learned colleagues!'

She heard a snort the other end. 'That man has no humility...no respect. He thumbs his nose at the conventions...he struts around like a peacock! And who is he? A nobody! A nobody from the bush. And the bush is where he still likes to bury himself—he has no time for the circles we move in. What kind of life d'you think he could offer a girl like you?'

'Daddy, we only had dinner together. A work-related dinner,' Tanya spelt out. No need to mention the other times they had seen each other outside the courtroom. Why upset her father unduly when she had probably seen Simon for the last time?

'You could do a lot worse than Bill Hendry's son James. Bill says he's——'

'James is a bore.' Pointless letting her father get his hopes up in that direction. 'I'm not interested.'

'I can't think why you dumped young Manning-Smith,' came the peevish response. 'There's a young man who's going places. He's presentable, well-off, ambitious...and he comes from a fine family.'

To her own surprise, she heard herself retorting, 'Simon's parents sound like fine people too, Daddy.'

Another snort. 'Well, they're hardly *our* type of people. What was wrong with young Manning-Smith anyway?' he persisted gruffly. 'He was crazy about you.'

'He stifled me. I couldn't breathe. He wanted to own me, body and soul.'

'What's wrong with that? He would have looked after you—given you everything you could possibly want. Isn't that what a girl wants from a man? To be the centre of his universe?'

'I didn't love him, Daddy.'

'Eh?'

'I didn't love Nick. I don't love Nick or James Hendry or...or anybody,' Tanya said, and felt a coldness as she said it.

She heard her father clicking his tongue. 'You do want to get married and have a family one day, don't you?'

'Of course...some day. Only when I do, I don't intend to be a social butterfly, caught up in endless lunches and charity functions.' Like Mother, she thought. 'I want to go on working.'

'Then you'd better forget Simon Devlin,' her father said brutally. 'He won't want a working wife. Or a city girl, for that matter. You must have heard the rumours that he's thinking of giving up the bar and moving back to the bush for good. Somehow I can't see you as a tree farmer's wife.'

'Daddy, I know all that,' Tanya said wearily. 'I have no intention of becoming a farmer's wife. Of being any kind of wife to Simon Devlin. Anyway, can you see him wanting to marry *me*? A daughter of the Establishment?' She gave a rather forced little trill of laughter, hoping to cajole her father out of his fears. As if he had any earthly need to worry! 'So let's drop it, shall we? You've raised your blood pressure for no reason.'

Her father gave a grunt, as if he wasn't entirely convinced. 'Well, it'll be good to see you. Here's your mother.'

Tanya hissed in her breath as her mother came back on the line. 'Mother, if I come over for lunch, you won't bombard me with questions about my love life, will you? My *non-existent* love life,' she stressed. 'I just want to relax, hear what *you've* been doing, talk about the trial, and then I'll come home and have a quiet night...'

'Of course we won't, dear. You know we only——'

'Mother, I must fly. I want to catch the market. See you around noon. That OK?' The second she heard her mother's answering 'That'll be fine, dear', Tanya rang off.

Her visit home didn't turn out to be the relaxing diversion she had hoped. Though both her parents were careful not to mention Simon Devlin's name, their unspoken questions hung in the air, creating tensions she could have done without. She left as soon as she decently could, pleading that she wanted an early night, and needed to do some ironing first.

Her ironing actually was disposed of in minutes, and with that out of the way she decided to make herself an omelette and then settle down to play her violin for a while. With Ellie away, she could play to her heart's content.

When her doorbell rang, her heart dipped. Please, not James Hendry, she begged silently.

Her heart did a complete somersault when she saw Simon Devlin on her doorstep, his great frame almost filling the doorway.

'Simon!' What was he doing back in town on a Saturday night? He had only gone bush this morning!

Why was he here at all, when there was no longer any reason for him to make contact? She found herself swallowing hard, trying to dislodge a sudden lump in her throat.

'Aren't you going to ask me in?'

'Sorry.' She moved swiftly aside. 'Come in . . . please.' Stay calm, for heaven's sake, she thought. It's probably something to do with work . . . with the costing for the trial . . . it could be anything.

'Something I can do for you?' she asked carefully. How polite she sounded, how cool and remote. Why couldn't she have come straight out and said in all sincerity, 'It's great to see you'?

A girl could make herself vulnerable that way, that was why.

'Maybe,' came the droll response. He sounded amused, as if he had seen right through her.

'I'm just making myself an omelette,' she said, turning away from him for her own self-preservation. 'Would you like one?'

'Please. Sounds good.'

He followed her into the kitchen, watching languidly as she worked.

'Planning a quiet night at home, are you?' he asked. He cocked an eyebrow at her when she nodded. 'I'm surprised. No night out on the town tonight? Or are you expecting company?'

'You seem to think I do nothing but kick up my heels. I was going to play my violin, as a matter of fact. Ellie's away for the weekend. And later I planned to settle down with a good book. Curled up on the sofa... Alone.'

'Alone? On a Saturday night? That doesn't sound like our high-living Tanya.'

'No, it doesn't, does it? I must be sickening for something.' Yes, but what? Physically, she felt fine.

'I hope not,' said Simon. 'I have an invitation for you—to the opening of an art show tonight at eight. It's just around the corner from here. Like to come along? Free cocktails and canapés thrown in.'

She felt a leap of pleasure—and surprise. 'I didn't know you went in for that kind of thing: being seen at openings, dodging society photographers...cocktail chitchat.'

'I don't. In this case, I happen to know the artist. I met him when he was painting the forests around my place. The theme of his show is the Gippsland forests. They say he can paint trees like no other artist in the country. He makes every trunk, every branch, every leaf leap off the canvas.'

Tanya felt flattered that Simon wanted her to go with him, when she had shown such an abysmal lack of interest so far in his own trees.

'I'd love to come,' she answered. 'I might learn something.' She said that deliberately, in unspoken apology for the way she had allowed her mind to wander in the past, each time Simon had tried to describe the different varieties of trees in his plantation, and in the forests round his home. And how lovingly he had described them, she realised now, thinking back. It was a wonder he was bothering to give her a second chance.

She did learn something from the art show. More than just 'something', and far more than she expected. In a short couple of hours she learned more about Australian native trees than she ever would have believed possible. And she learned something about herself too, though she buried that particular knowledge in the deepest recesses of her being for now, to examine at a later date...when she felt a little more secure in her new-found knowledge.

She wondered afterwards how a few painted trees could have so quickly and completely captivated her. Perhaps it was because this time she genuinely listened to Simon and absorbed what he had to say. This time she genuinely looked at the trees in front of her, making an effort to see them through Simon's loving eyes. And this time she saw, as she never had before, their true beauty and grandeur.

Or... she tried to be brutally honest with herself. Was her new-found appreciation more to do with Simon himself—because she was so conscious of him now that everything he said caught and held her interest, everything in his presence seemed imbued with a new and special fascination?

He was an intriguing man, charming, magnetic, amusing—a complex, multi-faceted, broad-thinking man, far different from the arrogant, derisive, opinionated chauvinist she had first taken him to be. Those traits were all a part of his make-up too, but they were surface things, the protective shield he chose to show the world. Underneath he had many fine qualities, and far more aspects to his character than he would ever show to a mere acquaintance.

By choosing to reveal himself to *her*, he was paying her a rare compliment. Could she count him as a friend now? She dared not conceive that he could ever be more than a friend. And yet—and yet——

No! Swiftly Tanya blocked out the dim hope that had surfaced. She mustn't even think along those lines. Whatever truths, whatever yearnings lay buried deep in her psyche, it would be foolish to delve into them now, so early in their... friendship. Friendship was probably all Simon would ever want of her. Why yearn for something that was highly unlikely ever to happen? Why yearn for something that could never lead anywhere?

Only—she bit her lip—now that her emotions were already stirred, how could she bear to remain 'just friends' with Simon? Just to be near him made her pulses leap. Even an accidental touch set her heart spiralling. What would she be like if one day he were to take her into his arms, not as he had done on those earlier occasions, playfully, carelessly, teasingly, merely taking advantage of a situation that offered, but this time because he had come to genuinely care for her and wanted a deeper relationship with her?

Would she be strong enough to push him away, knowing that an involvement with Simon could never lead to a serious, long-lasting commitment? Because she couldn't see Simon ever giving up his dream of living permanently in the bush...or even wanting to give up his weekends in the bush. And no more could she see herself wanting to give up her own way of life—her comfortable city lifestyle—to follow Simon into the wilds.

And yet, even knowing all that, knowing she had no future with Simon, how could she be sure any more that she would have the will-power to push him away, or even want to? Would the bliss of being in his arms, if only for a short time, be worth the pain and the heartache that would inevitably follow?

She sighed. In all likelihood, it was a dilemma she would never need to face. Because in all likelihood Simon would never care enough to want to put her to the test.

As Simon brought his car to a halt outside her flat, he twisted round to face her, sliding one arm behind her so that the tips of his fingers were trailing across the nape of her neck, doing magical things to her sensory nerves. The thought of dilemmas and tests flew out of the window as if they had never existed. It seemed the most natural thing in the world when his arm came down and curled round her shoulders, and it seemed just as natural to lean back against him and rest her head in the snug hollow between his neck and his shoulder.

Simon cupped his hand under her chin and gently tilted her head back, and that seemed perfectly natural too—if a trifle alarming at the same time. She waited, her heart skittering in her breast, knowing that he was going to kiss her, knowing she ought to stop it here and now, and yet knowing equally well that she was going to do nothing at all to stop him. There was a kind of paralysing inevitability about what was about to happen. She even raised her lips to meet his.

'Tanya,' he breathed, and then his mouth was on hers, stifling her breath, his lips warm and searching, sending spirals of ecstasy through her.

She moaned under the pressure of his lips, her own lips opening instinctively under his. She was startled at her eager, abandoned response, at the way she allowed his tongue to glide along her teeth and thrust deep inside, at the way she let her own tongue move against his. With Nick, she had always found deep kissing mildly distasteful, but she had put up with it because she had denied him other more intimate liberties. Now she recognised why she had found it distasteful. She hadn't cared for him enough, hadn't loved him enough...hadn't loved him at all!

Whereas... She began to tremble in Simon's arms. Did that mean...could it mean...? She jerked back her head, looking up at him dazedly as reality dawned, filling her with wonder and dismay. This was the very thing she had feared, had been warning herself against all along...against letting her emotions get involved, against *falling in love with Simon*. Dear heaven, what was she going to do?

Simon looked down at her for a long moment, his eyes liquid-dark and unreadable in the dimness. Had he sensed the turmoil inside her, guessed why she was retreating from him? His hand moved to her cheek, stroking it gently as if he understood, and wasn't offended. Or else he doesn't care, she thought bleakly. He must know as well as I do that it would be a mistake for us to start anything. It would only create difficulties. Insurmountable difficulties...

From somewhere deep inside her a despairing voice cried, I don't care about the difficulties... I'm beyond caring about anything at this moment but the fact that I'm in love with you...

She clamped her teeth down hard on her lip so that the cry couldn't escape. She wasn't completely lost yet!

'You'd better go in,' Simon advised gently, extricating himself. Had he seen the danger too?

Tanya flushed as she realised she had been clinging to him. 'Yes,' she answered huskily, 'I think maybe I'd better.'

As she threw open the car door to step out, he caught her arm, bringing her heart to her mouth.

'Come bush with me tomorrow. It's my mother's birthday and I'm having the family over for dinner tomorrow night...a barbecue. You'll have a chance to meet them all.'

She felt giddy. 'I'd...very much like to meet your family,' she heard herself saying.

'Then you'll come? I'll drive you back Monday evening. We'll have two days together.'

She nodded, gulping. Two whole days with Simon... She closed her mind to the danger, to the problems, to the heartache that could lie ahead.

'Bring a swimsuit,' he suggested with the ghost of a grin. 'If it's warm enough, you'll be able to have that swim you missed.' As quick apprehension flared in her eyes, he chuckled softly, 'Don't worry, I promise to keep

you safe from snakes...and spiders...and possums.'
Now there was faint mockery in his eyes.

'And who's going to keep me safe from *you*?' she retorted with a flare of her old spirit.

'You won't need any protecting from me,' he said,
dropping his taunting tone. 'I would never do anything
to hurt you...or anything you didn't want.' He stroked
her hair back from her face, his touch infinitely gentle.

Was this the same man, she wondered hazily, who had
seized her so carelessly on at least two occasions the last
time she had spent a weekend with him? But they had
barely known each other then. They had both been
cynical, thoughtless, antagonistic, full of misconceptions about each other...

'Then maybe I need protecting from myself,' she said
with a rueful tilt of her lip. 'I feel quite weak and limbless
when I'm around you. You...may have noticed. I—I
can't even think straight.'

'Then maybe you should just follow your instincts.'

She knew where her instincts would lead her. Into deep
trouble! But she had known all along that Simon Devlin
was trouble...and she had gone on seeing him regardless, knowing there would be problems ahead if she
let herself get involved with him.

'And bring your violin,' Simon suggested. 'We could
try our hand at a duet. Might be fun.'

It might, at that. 'Should I throw in my tennis racquet
as well?' It was beginning to sound like a fun weekend.
She would concentrate on that side of it—the fun part.
The emotional aspects she wouldn't even think about.

'Afraid the court's not finished yet. Keep your racquet
well sprung for later.'

Later...would there be a later? she wondered, her heart
squeezing with hope.

Take it a step at a time, she cautioned herself. This weekend is all that matters now...

Was Simon, by asking her back, hoping that this time she would make more of an effort to enjoy the place—would even grow to like it, the way he did? Would that be possible? Tanya felt a knot of disquiet growing in her stomach. If she still couldn't reconcile herself to Simon's beloved bush, and Simon saw that she couldn't, would he stop seeing her in the future?

'Give the place another chance,' he urged quietly, as if he were reading her mind. 'A fair trial, as we in the legal fraternity would say. No strings. No pressure. Just come and have a good time. And I hope you'll enjoy meeting my family at the same time.'

'I'm looking forward to it,' she said stoutly, pushing down her qualms. A step at a time...she must think no further ahead than that.

CHAPTER NINE

THE drive that had seemed so interminable the first time, in the blinding rain and the swirling darkness, with Simon a cold, hostile stranger alongside her, was, on this occasion, pure pleasure. They both chatted unrestrainedly, and whereas before the winding road through the forests had left Tanya feeling distinctly queasy, today she barely noticed the bends.

The fact that it was a bright sunny morning—a pleasant change from the steady rain of the past week—helped. It was a glorious day, the sky a clear deep blue, the air crisp, the hills already covered in a mantle of rich green after the recent rains, imbuing them with a new lush beauty—a far cry from the dry parched hills that had so depressed her the first time.

Each time they passed through a tract of forest, she made a game of identifying the different varieties of eucalypts, and Simon smiled rather than scolded when she made a mistake, and gently set her straight. In no time, it seemed, they were turning off the main highway on to the unsealed road that wound over the hills to Simon's property. She noticed a warning sign: 'Kangaroos next 5 K', and she asked Simon, 'Do you ever see any?'

'Often,' he said, nodding, 'but mostly at night. Kangaroos, and wombats too, occasionally. You need to drive carefully.'

Today there was no sign of any wildlife, and Tanya was vaguely disappointed. She had seen kangaroos and wombats often enough in sanctuaries and zoos, but never roaming free in the bush.

Before long they were passing through the open gates of Simon's property. Eventually, through the bright curtain of gums and wattles, she glimpsed his unusual home with its soaring lines and large windows and shady vine-clad pergolas.

Clinically, she examined her feelings, now that she was back here again. She felt excited...expectant...but still strangely alien, still unsure of herself and her surroundings. She wondered if the sight of Simon's house would ever make her feel that she was 'coming home'. At this point in time, she doubted it.

Inside, the place was welcoming. Brigitte—or Simon's sister Maggie—had obviously been in recently to clean up and arrange fresh flowers. Native flowers, as before. Tanya could put a name to some of them now, thanks to Simon. Grevilleas, sun orchids, banksias, melaleucas, sweet-smelling boronias... She felt quite proud of herself as she ticked them off in her mind.

'Like a swim before lunch?' Simon suggested from the kitchen doorway. Tanya had left him unpacking the steaks and fresh fruit they had bought on their way. As she turned, he grinned, 'You'll know to stick close to the path this time... Better still, stick close to me. And wear sneakers...you won't need boots if you stay on the path.'

'Yes, sir!' It sounded enticing...sticking close to Simon.

She trod warily, but there were no mishaps this time on the steepish descent to the river. She had secretly had reservations about Simon's rock pool, but she needn't have. The water was crystal-clear, and deliciously cool once she got over the first shock of diving into its icy depths. The pool had been carved out of the rocky hillside, obviously over a period of many years.

As they both surfaced, Simon caught her to him and kissed her, his hands moving the length of her back to draw her up closer against him in a caress that made the blood thunder in her ears. They clung to each other as they bobbed about up to their necks, water streaming from their hair and trickling down their faces.

It felt tantalisingly sensual kissing Simon this way, feeling his lips cool and wet on hers, feeling the full length of his body, naked but for a tiny strip of red cloth, in close contact with her own.

Tanya closed her eyes and arched against him as pleasurable little stabs shot down her body into the pit of her stomach, her taut breasts straining against his broad chest. Waves of ecstasy throbbed through her as she felt his hands on her lower back, pressing her even closer.

Next moment the water closed over their heads, and spluttering, they struggled to the surface, laughter defusing their passion—for now.

'You're getting cold,' said Simon as he dragged her on to the rocks. She didn't feel cold—certainly she wasn't cold inside, she was burning all through—though when she glanced down at her arms she saw that they were covered with tiny goosebumps.

Simon wrapped a towel round her, and she looked up into his face and saw that he was looking down into *hers* with a heart-stopping tenderness in his eyes—not the glazed, unseeing, self-centred desire that she had seen so often in Nick's eyes, but a far softer, more aware, more sharing expression.

She smiled involuntarily, and he smiled back, and it was as if they shared a delicious, unspoken secret. Tanya knew what her secret was. Was she only imagining that Simon felt the same?

They returned to the house to shower and change, and after a light lunch of canned pumpkin soup with fingers of toast smeared with Vegemite, and hot fresh coffee, they wandered out to the tree plantation, where Simon set to work on some tidying up and thinning out, content to have Tanya chat to him while he worked.

'Can't I help?' she asked after a while.

He straightened, eyeing her with a quizzical expression. 'Is that a rhetorical question—or do you mean it?'

'You still think I'm just a good-time girl, don't you?' she challenged, with a twinge of disappointment.

'No, I don't think that,' he denied, his tone serious now. 'Not at all. I've seen how hard you work at your job, and how committed you are to your profession. I've heard you discuss local and world affairs as if you genuinely care about a whole range of issues, including people less fortunate than yourself. Your concerns and your interests—and your talents too—are far broader than I ever would have imagined when I first met you. But even way back then...'

He paused, and there was something in his eyes now that made her heart miss a beat. 'Even then I must have sensed deep down that there was a lot more to you than appeared on the surface, because right from the start there was something about you that got to me...that got right under my skin. And people tell me I have a pretty tough skin.'

Tanya could feel herself blushing. It meant a lot to her to hear Simon declaring that he liked her for herself. Other men, she suspected, had been attracted more to her social position, to her family's wealth, to the way she looked and dressed, than to her as a person. Even Nick Manning-Smith had been more conscious of those shallow surface things, she realised now, than of her as a person with opinions and needs and feelings of her own.

She felt her skin tingle as Simon caught her hand. 'So you see...' he looked down at her with a rather sheepish smile, 'even when I believed you to be a pampered daddy's darling who'd always had everything handed to her on a platter, I've never been entirely immune to you. Now, of course...' He pulled her to him, 'any immunity I had left has been all shot to pieces.'

'Oh?' She gave him an arch look—not easy to achieve with her heart in such a flutter. 'How is that?' Spell it out, Simon, she thought. Tell me exactly what you feel for me, what you want of me. I need to know!

'A moment ago you offered to help me.' Smoothly, he sidestepped her question. 'If we stand around talking all day, neither of us will do any work at all.'

So he wasn't ready to commit himself yet. Was he still not sure? Of himself? Of her? Or was he thinking of all the difficulties they would have to face up to once they did declare how they felt? Or did he simply want to give them both a little more time? Time to be quite sure...'A fair trial' was the way he had described this weekend.

OK. She would give it a fair trial. She would keep an open mind. She would try really hard to like Simon's bush world.

But she still couldn't see herself ever wanting to come and live here. Simon, if he was beginning to care for her the way she cared for him, would surely, for her sake, agree to stay in town... Wouldn't he?

*   *   *

Tanya couldn't believe the day had passed so quickly. Or believe how hard she had worked! Side by side with Simon, she had helped to weed the plantation and then to check the fences, and later, while Simon dug over the vegetable garden, she had picked lettuces and tomatoes and dug up carrots and potatoes to make into salads for tonight's dinner.

And now, with Simon's family due to descend on them at any moment, Simon stood her in front of him, his strong warm hands on her shoulders, looking her up and down in a way that she wished he wouldn't—not just now, with his mother about to walk in!

'You look wonderful,' he said, approving of her mauve silk blouse and flared black skirt, and noting how her cheeks were healthily flushed and her eyes a clear sparkling violet. 'You look as fresh as a daisy. I thought you'd be dead on your feet.'

'Amazing what a hot shower can do,' she said, thinking that if he went on looking at her like that they would both be in mortal need of a *cold* shower!

'You're quite a worker,' he said. He was surprised... and she couldn't blame him. She had surprised herself. She would never have thought that she would find physical work—*farm* work, for heaven's sake!—so satisfying.

'That's high praise—from you,' she retorted. No need to get carried away simply because she had survived one afternoon in the bush—actually working! The work had really been a means to an end. She had wanted to be near Simon. That was why she hadn't really noticed how hard she had been working.

But she knew in all honesty that she *had* noticed the work—her palms were still smarting, her arms were scratched and sore, and her shoulders were aching! And yet she didn't care a bit! It *had* given her a sense of satisfaction, as if she had achieved something she hadn't thought possible. And yes, she had even enjoyed it!

'Here they are now.' Simon turned his head at the sound of a car in the drive. 'Ready?'

Tanya smiled. 'Ready.'

It was a surprisingly pleasant evening. Not that Tanya hadn't been expecting Simon's family to be pleasant, but she had never dreamed that they would make her feel so at ease, so much at home. There was no gushiness, no brittle attempt to impress, no sign either, thank goodness, that they were in any way awed by *her*. She was very quickly made to feel like one of the family.

Simon's father Matt was huge, a bear of a man, as she had imagined he would be. But, despite his years as a timber cutter, there was nothing loud, nothing rough or coarse about him. His speech was gentle, his manner courteous, and the pale blue eyes in his weatherbeaten face were sincere and warm. A true gentle giant.

Nellie, Simon's mother, was small, wiry and full of energy, despite the crippling arthritis visible in both hands. She had smoky grey eyes—Simon's eyes—striking silver hair, and was well-spoken and articulate, her voice surprisingly refined for someone who had, presumably, lived all her life in the bush.

Only she hadn't, Tanya discovered. 'She was a teacher,' Simon confided at one point, when they had a moment to themselves. 'She was sent out here from the city to teach at the local primary school. That's how she met my father. They fell in love, married within weeks, and have lived here happily ever since.'

Tanya's eyes widened. 'You mean your mother was a city girl?' He had never mentioned it before.

Simon cocked an eyebrow at her. 'That's what gives me hope,' he said. 'The knowledge that city girls can adapt to the bush.'

She swallowed. Was he just kidding her along, to see what reaction he'd get? Or did he seriously hope that in time she would come to like the bush enough—to care for *him* enough—to agree to live out here permanently?

'Didn't your mother miss the city? Her friends? Her family?' Unwittingly, revealingly, the questions popped out. 'What about the theatre? Concerts? Shopping? Things like that?' If she was giving away her own doubts, her own hopes, so be it. Perhaps it was best that Simon knew.

For a long moment he stood looking down at her, but his expression was strangely shuttered, impossible to read. 'If she did, she never said so,' he answered at length. 'She was an only child—her mother died when she was quite young, and her father was the only relative she had left in Melbourne. She used to go and visit him sometimes, and once or twice he came up here to stay with us. He died of a heart attack the year Maggie was born.'

'I suppose with her father gone it would have made it easier for her to cut her ties with the city,' Tanya said musingly. But surely there must have been other things about the city that his mother had missed!

'I think she loved my father so much she would have followed him anywhere. She gave up her old city life without a qualm—friends, family, everything.' Though Simon spoke mildly, his eyes softening as he spoke, Tanya felt vaguely reprimanded. Was he implying that he would expect her to give up everything for him, if and when they declared their love?

She bit her lip. She did love Simon. She loved him and wanted him and needed him—yes, *needed*, she realised in astonishment—as she had never loved or wanted or needed any other man.

But she still wasn't sure that she would be prepared to give up everything she knew and loved, her job, her family, her city lifestyle, the way Simon's mother had, and meekly follow Simon into the bush to live. Would Simon understand, and agree to a compromise? Or would he accuse her of not loving him enough, and wash his hands of her?

Why can't the man be the one to follow the woman? her heart cried in silent protest. Simon has proved that he can live quite happily in the city... But however hard I try, the bush is always going to be an alien place to me!

'How about playing us some Chopin, Simon?' Nellie called out, and Simon's sister Maggie cried, 'Oh, yes, please, Simon! The boys love it when you play.' Maggie had her father's pale blue eyes and her mother's vitality, and had treated Tanya all evening like a friend—or a sister.

Her two young sons came bounding over and dragged Simon off to the piano. After he had obliged with a couple of Preludes and Mazurkas, he persuaded Tanya to fetch her violin, and after flicking through their respective music scores, they found a couple of pieces they felt confident enough to play together. Their impromptu performance was a hit, judging by the wild applause and the catcalls, and Simon, grinning, seized Tanya round the waist and, in full view of his entire family, planted a kiss full on her lips.

'That was fun,' he said, and she wondered if he meant the performance—or the kiss. Both, she thought dreamily. Playing together had certainly been great fun. It had, in fact, been a fun night—far more fun, she realised, than a lot of the parties she had been to in town. She recalled the meaningless small-talk, the drinking, the smarting smoke in the eyes, the blaring disco music drowning out conversation. You've changed, Tanya Barrington, she reflected with a rueful smile. Simon Devlin has done this to you. You'd better watch out, or soon he'll have you doing whatever he wants!

It was with that thought in mind that she was able to keep her head later, when Simon, after seeing his family off, took her into his arms and crushed his mouth to hers—not the way he had earlier in the evening, light-heartedly, with his amused family looking on, but this time with a fierce passion burning in his eyes and a reckless hunger in his marauding lips that warned her he could, this time, be dangerously close to losing control.

Knowing she would be lost if he did, she twisted round, tearing her mouth away. 'Simon, no!' she gasped. 'Please...not—not now!'

'What's wrong?' She saw the desire ebbing from his eyes, and swift concern taking its place.

'I—I'm afraid.'

'Afraid?' He looked at her in astonishment. 'Of me?'

'No—I don't know. Of me. Of...what might happen.' Of what might happen if I lose my willpower on top of already losing my heart...

'Ah,' he said, and she realised with a start that he was thinking of something quite different—something she, foolishly, hadn't even considered. She stifled a sigh. There was so much to think about these days...safe sex, unwanted pregnancy, let alone the danger of losing one's ability to think, to act wisely.

'You're right.' He was already drawing away, gently, reluctantly. 'When you agreed to come for the weekend, I promised I'd keep you safe, didn't I?' His lip quirked. 'I was thinking of outsiders, intruders, venomous creatures . . . not of myself. Forgive me. It was never my intention to rush you into anything . . . to do anything you didn't want, I swear.'

'Simon, I wasn't thinking about . . . about being safe,' she admitted, casting around for the right words. 'I was thinking about—about the way you make me *feel*. I was afraid I might lose my head and—and do something, say something I—I . . .' She shook her head, appealing to him with her eyes. 'I can't think properly when you're—when you're——'

He hushed her with a finger to her lips. 'It's all right,' he said gently. 'I understand. I want you, Tanya...heaven knows I want you desperately. I'm burning up for you. I need you as I've never needed any other woman. But I can wait. Because what I feel for you is more than just a physical need . . .' His finger fell away, and suddenly he was gripping her shoulders as if he would never let her go.

'Damn it, Tanya, I can't hold it back any longer . . . You must know by now how I feel about you. I'm in love with you!'

His eyes blazed into hers, jolting her with the power of the emotion she saw there. Shaken, Tanya stared back at him, for the first time feeling confident enough to let her own love shine freely from her eyes.

'Simon, I——'

'Hush now . . .' His finger was back on her lips. 'I'm just letting you know that my intentions are honourable,' he said with a glimmer of a smile. 'I love you and

I want you—I want you desperately. But I'm not looking for an affair. I'll want far more from you than that...'

Is he talking about marriage? she wondered dazedly. What else could he mean? The realisation was followed by the agonised question: *Could we make it work?*

He brought his hand up and swept her soft hair away from her face. 'We're going to have a few things to work out...I realise that. But there's no hurry, no pressure on us. The answers will come,' he said confidently, with a tenderness that threatened to melt every bone in her body. 'Now I'm going to let you go off to bed—alone,' he said regretfully—and firmly. 'I want you to keep a clear head,' he added with a tender smile. 'Sleep tight, my love. And if you hear any noises in the night, be an angel and ignore them. I don't think I could stand the strain if you came into my room again in the middle of the night. I'm only flesh and blood, after all!'

'Same here,' she said with a sigh, and slipped away from him before either of them could forget their high-minded intentions.

There was no sign of Simon when Tanya emerged from her room the next morning around eight o'clock, refreshed and eager to be with him for another precious day. He had probably been up for hours! Instead of going looking for him, she started preparing his breakfast.

When he strode in, kicking off his heavy work boots on his way in, she felt her heart twist inside her with love and longing. He gave her a smile that made her feel quite giddy.

'Have a good night?' he asked, dropping a kiss on her brow—as a returning husband might, she thought breathlessly, after a morning in the fields.

'Slept like a top,' she said, smiling. And dreamt all night long about you, she added silently.

'I had a restless night,' he admitted. 'It was unsettling not having a visit from you in the middle of the night. Not even a distant scream!' His eyes were teasing.

'You're never going to let me live that weekend down, are you?' Tanya grinned back.

'Never.'

They laughed, easy, shared laughter. It felt good. They spent the rest of the morning working side by side in the plantation, and they chatted and grew closer as they worked.

When they stopped for lunch, they prepared it together, and ate it outside on the shady patio. Just as they were finished, they heard a car in the drive. Maggie? Brigitte? Tanya looked at Simon.

'Let's go and see.' He reached for her hand.

It was Dimity Donohue. Her bright smile of greeting faltered when she saw Tanya, and faded altogether when she noticed their linked hands.

'I didn't realise you had…company,' she said, making the word sound almost like an insult. 'I brought you some almonds.' She waved a paper bag at Simon.

'Thanks, Dimity. Join us for coffee?' he invited. He hadn't dropped Tanya's hand, and it warmed her that he hadn't.

'No, thanks. Two's company, three's a crowd. Be seeing you.' Thrusting the bag of almonds at Simon, Dimity turned on her heel, jumped into her car, and drove off.

Tanya looked enquiringly at Simon. 'She seems upset. I think she has designs on you.'

He shrugged. 'Well, I've never given her any encouragement. I told you once that rabid feminists weren't my cup of tea. I can tolerate them in a work context, or even as a neighbour. But in my private life—no, thanks. I admire Dimity's intellect, her drive, her dedication to her work. But personally, she leaves me cold.'

Tanya felt relief wash over her. She smiled at Simon, her heart feeling a few pounds lighter.

Simon looked down at her. 'You look irresistible when you smile like that. Come here.' Next moment she was in his arms, reeling under his slow, drugging kisses, hypnotised by the touch of his hands as they explored the soft lines of her back, her waist, her hips, feeling weak and giddy and blissfully happy in the conviction that the love they felt for each other would be strong enough to conquer any problems they would have to face.

'There is no other woman,' Simon breathed into her hair. 'There hasn't been since the day I first met you. There is only you, my love. There will never be anyone but you. We'll work things out . . . you'll see.'

Tanya nodded. She was beginning to believe him.

It was late when Simon dropped her off at her flat, and her phone was ringing. It was her father.

'I thought you were having a quiet weekend at home,' he grumbled.

'I——' She hesitated. Then she made up her mind. He had to know some time. 'Simon asked me to meet his family, Daddy. I've been up bush for a couple of days.'

She waited for the explosion, and was surprised, and a little suspicious, when it didn't come. After a moment of silence her father said only, 'How about meeting me for lunch tomorrow? We haven't had lunch together for ages—just the two of us, I mean.'

She knew she would have to go. There were things she had to tell him, prepare him for...things she couldn't tell him over the phone.

'Where and when?' she asked.

'Fanny's. Twelve-thirty.' He rang off.

With a sigh, Tanya replaced the receiver. She wasn't looking forward to this lunch.

Her father had booked a secluded table, a bountiful floral display providing added privacy. An ominous sign, Tanya thought, taking a deep breath before she sat down.

A few blessed moments were spent perusing the menu and choosing a bottle of wine. French wine. Lobster. Caviar. Her father wasn't stinting himself today. It wasn't until their meal was placed before them and the waiter had melted away that her father finally laid his cards on the table.

'How serious are you about this Devlin character?' Her father was never one to beat about the bush. Not when the time came to strike.

'His name is Simon, Daddy.' She picked up her glass of wine and sipped long and slowly, determined to keep calm.

'Simon, then.' He too was holding himself in check with a visible effort. There were red spots high on his cheeks. They alarmed her. If his blood pressure was up, she didn't want to send it through the roof.

'I love him, Daddy.' She spoke gently but firmly, appealing to him with all the power of her violet-blue eyes. 'And he loves me. I couldn't imagine my life without him now.'

She felt rather than saw her father flinch. He was still making a determined effort to maintain his icy self-control. 'You mean you're having an affair?' He was hoping that was all it was. That it would blow over, in time.

'I mean that we love each other and want to get married, Daddy. Have children. The whole bit.' She saw her father's head jerk back at the bald words, and assured him hastily, 'We're not rushing into anything. We both know that we have things to work out first.' She reached a hand across the table, but he didn't take it. 'I would dearly like to know I have your support, Daddy. Yours and Mother's.' She looked beseechingly at him.

It was a moment or two before he spoke. When he did, his voice was gravelly, a sign of the deep emotion he was still trying to control.

'I hope he hasn't fooled you into thinking he'll stay here in town. Once he has that ring on your finger, he'll put the pressure on you to go bush with him. Can you see yourself living buried in the bush?'

'Daddy, that's something we have to work out for ourselves. Simon hasn't tried to hide anything from me. He's been quite open about the fact that he would like to live and work in the country—but only if I want it too. We might even start up a law practice together...out of town somewhere.' She and Simon had tossed ideas at each other all afternoon...feeling their way, avoiding coming to any firm or final decisions. It was early days yet.

At her father's shocked look, she added quickly, 'On the other hand, we might simply go on the way we are now...living and working here in town, and just going bush at weekends.' Her own hopes injected a pensive note into her voice that her father was quick to exploit.

'You really believe he'd be content with that? He'd come to resent it in time...and you,' he said brutally.

'Then we'd have to look at our position again,' she said, wanting her father to know that whatever they decided to do, and wherever they decided to live, it would be a joint decision. *Theirs*. No one else's.

'What, and meekly follow him into the bush?' Her father's patience was wearing thin, she could read the signs. 'How could you give up everything you have here?' he demanded testily. 'All this...' He waved a hand, and she knew why he had brought her here to Fanny's for lunch, why he was showering her with lobster and caviar and French wine. 'You're a city girl...you've always been a city girl, through and through. You're not built for the isolation and hardship of the bush. How much do you know about his family?' he asked abruptly.

Tanya frowned at his choice of words. Not, 'Have you met his family?' but, 'How much do you know about them?', as if the most important thing about a family was their pedigree—a dubious factor here, in her father's eyes.

'They're nice people, Daddy,' she said, maintaining her poise with an effort. 'You'd like them.' If you'd only give them half a chance, she added under her breath.

He grunted. 'They're not our kind of people.'

'No,' she agreed, with a dryness she hoped wouldn't escape her father. 'They're warm, genuine, down-to-earth people, Daddy. Fine people.'

'They'd have been on their best behaviour, of course.' There was a faint sneer in her father's voice. 'Naturally they would want to impress you. You'd be quite a catch.'

She sucked in her breath. 'They're not like that, Daddy. Money and position don't impress them in the least.' She added deliberately, 'I couldn't hope for a more worthy family to marry into.'

A cold glint appeared in her father's eyes. 'You know nothing about them—obviously. You take it from me, my dear, they're not desirable people.'

Well, now the gloves were off in earnest!

Tanya's eyes narrowed angrily. 'What do you mean?' She knew her father was a snob. He'd always been one. But there seemed to be more here to her father's disapproval than mere snobbery, or the fact that Simon wanted to whisk her off into the wild blue yonder. She realised she was holding her breath.

'Has he told you about his brother?' rasped her father.

'His brother?' Tanya blinked. She cast back into her memory. 'You mean Christopher?'

'You've met him?' His voice was sharp.

'No, I haven't. He lives in Adelaide. What about him?' she asked, frowning. How did her father know about Simon's brother? she wondered, an uneasy knot coiling inside her.

'The man's a convicted criminal. An arsonist. He's been in gaol.'

Tanya gasped. Simon had mentioned some 'bad luck', she recalled. He had glossed over it, as if it had been nothing of consequence. Why hadn't he told her the truth, prepared her, so that she could have supported him now instead of sitting here, gaping at her father in obvious total ignorance? Now her father would know that Simon had been hiding things from her—that he had skeletons in his closet that he had chosen not to share with her. *Why* hadn't he? Because he was ashamed? Because he had thought it might tarnish his image in her eyes? Didn't he know her well enough, believe in her enough, *trust* her enough by now, to know that it wouldn't have made any difference?

'How do you know about Christopher?' she asked her father in a taut voice.

'I know about him because I was the barrister who defended him at his trial. There were two others charged with him. Drunken young hooligans, the lot of 'em. They vandalised a rival football team's clubhouse and then set fire to it. And after they were arrested, they all tried to blame each other. A charming bunch!'

Tanya gulped. She felt rather faint. 'Did—did Christopher plead guilty?'

Her father gave a snort. 'None of them admitted to anything. Devlin, who was my client, spun a tale about passing out in the car and not even knowing the damage was being done. That was our defence—for what it was worth. The trouble was, one of his mates spun the same story—vowed that *he* was asleep in the car and that *Devlin* was with the other guy. And the third one said he was too drunk to remember a thing, and wouldn't have been capable of even getting out of the car.'

'How did they come to be arrested in the first place?' Tanya asked, her lawyer's brain mercifully helping her to achieve a certain detachment.

'They were virtually caught in the act. They were so drunk, they crashed their car into a tree as they were speeding away from the burning clubhouse, and they were arrested on the spot. Open and shut case,' her father said with a grunt. 'Still, I did my best for Devlin. As I've always done for all my clients, no matter who they are or how disagreeable the case.'

'What was his sentence?' asked Tanya.

'Nine months. It could have been a lot more. The other two got longer because they'd had prior convictions.'

'So this was Christopher's first offence...'

'It certainly was not. He'd been up on a charge before—car theft. But he got off that time with a bond.' Repugnance laced her father's words. 'And this is the brother of the man you want to marry! I don't want you getting mixed up with that family,' he said bluntly.

'Christopher has obviously rehabilitated himself.' Tanya cast around for a line of defence. 'And it must have happened a long time ago. You can't hold a thing like that against a man forever...or against the rest of his family.'

'The weakness is there—in the family,' her father said harshly. 'Decently brought up children don't turn to crime.'

Tanya sighed. Her father, with his vast experience of crime and criminals, must know in his heart of hearts that that wasn't necessarily true. But she knew she wasn't going to convince him in this particular instance. If only Simon had told her the truth about Christopher, had put her fully into the picture, she might have been able to put up a better defence!

'I'd better get back to work,' she said tonelessly.

'You haven't had any dessert.' Belatedly, her father reached for her hand, but she had withdrawn it some time before.

'I've had enough, thanks,' she said. Enough of everything, for one day! 'Thank you for lunch, Daddy. It was lovely.' Lovely? Ha! 'I'd better fly—I have to be in court this afternoon.'

Her father rose too, his eyes troubled now, his face more florid than ever. 'Your mother and I love you, baby. We only want——'

'I know, Daddy,' she said, her tone gentler now. They only wanted what was best for her. And what was most comfortable for them. She stretched up to kiss his cheek. However right or wrong her father's motives might be, she had never doubted his love. Or his concern for her.

CHAPTER TEN

TANYA was in a fever of impatience, waiting for Simon to meet her after work, as they'd arranged the night before. But she didn't bring up the subject that was uppermost in her mind until they were sipping their coffee after the casual steak and salad meal she had prepared for him at her flat. Ellie had gone to dinner at her parents' place.

'Simon, why didn't you tell me about Christopher having been in gaol?' The question popped out, and it was all wrong. She hadn't intended to broach it that way. She had intended to lead into the subject of Christopher gradually. Damn, she thought. Now Simon will think that I'm worried about the fact that his brother was once a convicted criminal.

'Your father told you about Chris?' Was that faint surprise in his eyes? She couldn't read any more than that from his expression. It was strangely shuttered, keeping his thoughts locked up tight.

She nodded. 'Over lunch today. Simon, I wish you'd told me about him yourself. It wouldn't have caught me so off guard then. It wouldn't have looked as if—as if you were hiding things from me. *Why didn't you tell me?*'

Simon stared into his coffee-cup. Was he trying to avoid her eye? In a flash, the answer came to her. 'You were trying to save my feelings, was that it? Because it was my father who defended Christopher in court, and he didn't succeed in getting your brother off...'

Simon glanced up. His expression was still closed, still wary. 'That's about it,' he agreed with a shrug. 'I was trying to save your feelings... Why rake up the past, anyway?'

He smiled at her then, a gentle, beguiling smile, but there was something oddly strained about it, and there was an odd inflection in his voice. There was more to this than he was telling her. She knew Simon pretty well by now. Her love for him had made her sensitive to his moods, to changes in his tone, to his every passing expression. And he was hiding something from her. *Once again* he was hiding something from her! She was sure of it.

'Simon, don't let's have secrets from each other,' she begged. 'We can't start off a life together that way. We have to be honest and open with each other. I can take it, whatever it is. I love you.'

He looked at her for a long moment, his eyes tender, and troubled at the same time. 'How much did your father tell you?' he asked.

'He said your brother and two of his mates were charged with vandalising and setting fire to some clubrooms. They were all found guilty and sent to gaol.' Tanya didn't add the bit about them being 'drunken hooligans'. She was anxious to save Simon's feelings too.

Simon stretched his long legs out in front of him. She heard him heave a deep sigh as he did so. 'Christopher should never have been sent to gaol,' he said heavily. 'He should never have been convicted. He was innocent.'

'You mean he really *was* asleep in his car when the other two were vandalising the clubrooms?' Tanya felt a coldness down her spine. The implication was beginning to strike her. If Christopher was truly innocent...

'That's what he has always sworn to be the truth—
and I've never had any cause to doubt him,' Simon said,
his voice hard. 'Chris is no liar. The other two were the
ones who were lying—trying to save their own necks. If
they'd been cross-examined a bit harder in court, they
might have broken down and admitted the truth.'

'You mean...if your brother's barrister—*my father*—
had cross-examined them a bit harder...' Tanya re-
phrased it slowly, her face pale. 'Isn't that what you're
saying?'

Simon's hesitation was damning.

'You're saying my father didn't *try* hard enough?' she
demanded, her eyes dangerously narrowed.

He felt for her hand, but she snatched it away. 'Tanya
darling, it was a long time ago. Seventeen, eighteen
years...'

'But you still blame my father!' she accused.

There was an uncomfortable pause. She didn't realise
how hard she was clenching her fists until her fingernails
pierced the skin, almost drawing a cry from her.

'Look,' Simon appealed to her, 'I was a schoolboy at
the time, an impressionable schoolboy. It was my first
time ever in a courtroom. I went with my mother because my father had to work. I probably only imagined
that your father...' He let the words trail off, his mouth
tightening.

'That he—*what*, Simon?' Tanya almost screamed the
words at him. Indignation, pain, and a rush of protective love for her father brought a shrillness to her
voice. '*Tell* me!'

Simon pulled his legs in again, as if he felt he might
shortly be in need of their support. She saw his chest
heave. 'All right. I felt he rushed the case. I had the
impression—rightly or wrongly—that he didn't care what

happened to Christopher, that he had better things to do with his time than defend people like him, a nobody from the bush. I even saw him glance at his watch a few times.'

Tanya recoiled as if stung. Her father might not have cared much for Christopher as a person, but he had cared passionately about him as a client. Whether Chris had come from the bush or the city—whether he was a 'somebody' or not—wouldn't have come into it. Her father had done his best for him. He had said so.

'My father never gave less than his best—ever!' she cried vehemently. 'He always prided himself on his fairness, his dedication to *every* client he represented. Your brother was no exception!'

'No?' Simon sounded more sad than angry. Perhaps it was because he realised they were having their first fight. A fight that went deep to the core of both of them. 'I just felt he could have made more of an effort...taken more time...tried harder to break down the other two and make them admit the truth.'

'One of the others told the same story as Christopher,' she reminded him heatedly. 'Are you so sure your brother *was* telling the truth? Do you have any proof?'

'I don't need any proof. I know Chris.'

Tanya sighed. 'You said it happened a long time ago. If Chris was telling the truth, surely one of the others would have relented by now and backed up his story?'

'What, and risk a charge of perjury? Admit they'd set him up? They're hard cases, those two. They were back in gaol almost as soon as they were out.'

'Yes—*hard cases*!' She leapt on the phrase, her eyes flashing. 'And yet you expected my father to be able to break them down in court!'

He turned to her then, and the distress in his eyes sent a shaft of pain knifing through her. He was suffering at this moment as much as she, she realised. Not only from what had happened to his brother all those years ago, but from what was happening here now... to *them*.

She said in a tight voice, in defence of her father, 'My father said it wasn't your brother's first offence. He'd been up on another charge before—car theft. He was no saint!'

A sudden icy contempt flashed in Simon's eyes. 'A stupid, boyish prank! Chris got in with a wild young crowd when he first left home. They weren't bad kids—they were high-spirited rather than bad. Chris and a couple of the other kids found an unlocked car one night and took it for a ride. It was just a juvenile prank—to them. It was sheer bad luck that they were caught when they returned it. Then again, maybe it wasn't such bad luck. Chris swore, when he was let off with a bond, that he'd never get into trouble again.' The meaning behind his words was plain.

'Well, what was he doing with those two hooligans, then?' asked Tanya scathingly. 'Vandals. Arsonists!'

'They were just members of his football club, as far as Chris was concerned,' Simon said tartly. 'They'd been drinking together after a footy Grand Final, and Chris was drunk enough to agree to drive the other two around to the rival team's clubrooms after their own club closed up for the night. When they found the place already locked up and deserted, Chris's two drinking mates got mad and swore they were going to find a way in and help themselves to a drink. Drunk as he was, Chris wasn't having any of that, and he went back to his car, where he promptly passed out. He only found out what the other two had done after they leapt into his car, pushed him aside and then crashed the car as they sped off.'

'But one of the others told the same story he did!' Tanya argued. 'And you're blaming my father for not being able to hammer the truth out of him!'

'Not exactly. I'm blaming him—that is, I *did* blame him at the time—for not seeming to care. For not making more of an effort.'

She drew in a ragged breath. 'Your mother didn't mention having met my father,' she recalled, her voice half sad, half bitter. 'Is that because she feels the same way you do? Does she blame my father too?'

Simon shook his head. 'No.' It was an emphatic no. 'Sure, it was a very painful time for my mother, a time she would rather forget. But she never blamed your father. Never. She was grateful, if anything. One of the city's top barristers, coming out to a country town to defend her son...' A subtle change came into his voice, edging his words with bitterness. 'She was determined to have the best defence for Chris. To raise enough money to engage a good barrister, she even sold her grand piano—her most precious possession.'

'She sold her piano?' Tanya's face blushed. 'But Simon, isn't it in your——'

'I managed to buy it back, years later.' Simon's eyes were hard. 'But by then she wasn't capable of playing any more and insisted that I keep it.'

Simon must have felt deeply for his mother at the time she sold it, Tanya reflected painfully. What an enormous sacrifice on his mother's part. Her beloved piano! How she must have missed it in the days when she was still capable of playing.

She slumped forward, her shoulders bowed, her soft hair spilling across her cheeks. How could she and Simon ever come together after this? she wondered bleakly. How could their *families* ever come together after this? There would always be doubts, reproaches, bitterness, regrets.

She felt Simon's hand on her shoulder, and much as she wanted to respond, to lay her cheek on his hand, she couldn't. She felt numbed. 'I need time to think,' she mumbled, without looking up. 'Please go now, Simon. Please . . . just go.'

An agonising silence fell between them. Then she felt him move, heard him heave himself to his feet. A wild panic washed over her, and she almost reached up to drag him back.

But she didn't. Pride, hurt, and the numbness which was still paralysing her, held her back. She wondered if things would ever come right, if she and Simon could ever recapture the closeness they had had before, so briefly. At this moment, it seemed unlikely.

'I just want you to know this,' said Simon as he turned to leave. His voice was flat, totally devoid of emotion. Or was he simply holding it in rein? 'Regardless of whether the impression I had all those years ago was a true impression or not, I've come to know your father in recent years as a fine barrister, and a fine judge. I'm deeply sorry if by bringing this all up now I have put doubts into your mind.'

Her loyalty to her father made her cry out then, lashing back at him angrily. 'I have no doubts about my father! You were obviously mistaken . . . You said yourself you were just a boy. The impressionable younger brother!' She buried her head in her hands. 'Leave me, Simon . . . *please.*'

She didn't look up until she heard the front door click shut behind him. She raised her head then, and sat for

a long time staring into space, tormenting herself by
going over and over all that Simon had told her.

She thought she understood now why Simon had
chosen to become a barrister. She had always suspected
that there had been more to his decision than a mere
wish to make money. At the time of his brother's trial,
Simon must have been at an age when he would have
had to think about choosing a career. She could imagine
him as he must have been at that time, a young lad,
pained, full of ideals, disillusioned by what had happened to his brother, hurt by the big city barrister's
failure to save his brother from gaol. Had he vowed then
to become a barrister himself one day, so that ordinary
folk like his brother could engage the services of a barrister who cared about them, who would fight to the
bitter end for them?

But her father *had* cared! Her heart twisted in outraged agony. He had always cared about his clients, rich
and poor alike!

Hadn't he?

Tanya groaned. Damn Simon Devlin! He *had* put
doubts into her mind! Not intentionally, she conceded.
He hadn't wanted to say anything at all—she had had
to drag all this out of him. And then when he had reluctantly unburdened himself, she had turned on him
and ordered him out. Out of her *life*, Simon must be
thinking.

Her lips twisted at the painful irony of it. If she never
saw Simon again she supposed her father would be
happy. He'd never approved of Simon. Simon didn't fit
into her father's well-ordered, snobbish, conservative city
world—and worse, he wanted to take his precious
daughter away and 'bury her' in the bush.

How ironic if Simon's honesty tonight were to give her father what he wanted. Worse than ironic—tragic! 'Simon, I can't lose you now—I won't!' she vowed hoarsely. And yet how could she and Simon ever come to terms with any of this unless she had it out with her father first, heard *his* side, and then went back and thrashed it out with Simon? Simon wanted to believe he was mistaken...it would be a relief to him if she could assure him that he had been.

But how was she going to broach such a delicate matter with her father? Tanya shuddered at the thought. Her father would be furious with Simon; he would accuse him of trying to blacken him in his beloved daughter's eyes; he would never forgive Simon!

What was she going to do?

On an impulse, she picked up the phone.

'Mother, can I come over and sleep at your place tonight? Ellie's not home yet and I—I don't feel like being alone.'

'Of course, darling, come on over.' Her mother didn't ask any question over the phone, but as soon as Tanya arrived, she put an arm round her shoulder, drew her into the den, and asked tentatively, 'Won't you tell me what's wrong, dear?'

Tanya hesitated. She thought of fobbing her mother off with a lie, pleading a headache, a stomach ache, anything to avoid telling her the truth, but she couldn't do it, she couldn't hold it back. It all poured out, everything she and her father had said over lunch, everything Simon had reluctantly told her earlier tonight.

And just as she finished, she heard a movement behind her and she turned, in horror, to see her father standing in the doorway.

'D-Daddy?' She ran to him, distress in her eyes, noting in dismay that the red spots were back in his cheeks and that there was a pulse throbbing at his temple. He looked old—old and defeated rather than angry. Dear lord, what had she done!

He held up a hand. For a second he looked past Tanya at her mother.

'Seventeen years ago,' he said in a strange, haunted voice, quite unlike his own. 'You remember that day, Ann? There was a country trial…remember? All I could think about was getting back to town…' His voice cracked. 'Maybe I did hustle things along that day, but I——'

Tanya's mother ran to him and grasped his arm. 'It's all right, dear…don't distress yourself. Tan will understand.'

'You mean—it's *true*?' Tanya's eyes had widened in shock.

Her father turned to her then, with appeal in his eyes. 'I never thought that what I did would affect the outcome of the trial—it seemed an open and shut case. If it hadn't been, I would have asked for an adjournment. Or handed the case over to somebody else.'

'But it wasn't an open and shut case, Daddy,' she burst out. 'You heard what I just told Mother. Simon's brother was innocent! He really was asleep in his car when the crime was being committed. The other two were the ones who were lying—not Christopher.'

Her father seemed to rally for a moment. 'Naturally a loyal schoolboy brother would believe whatever his older brother told him. Even if it's true—what you say— it would have been well-nigh impossible to prove it in court, with the other two sticking to their own stories and refusing to budge.'

'But if you'd applied more pressure...taken more time...forced the truth out of them?' The questions were wrenched from her, the hardest questions she had asked in her life.

Her father's face contorted with pain. 'Maybe...maybe. I've often wondered.'

Tanya gulped. Quite a confession for her father! She had thought him invincible. '*Why* didn't you take more time, Daddy?' she pressed. Why was he in such a hurry to get back to town? To go to a dinner? To go to his club?

He reached out his hand, and she let him take it, let him draw her closer. She saw his love for her shimmering behind the agony in his eyes.

'It was because of you, baby. I was worried sick about *you*.'

She blinked at him. '*Me?*'

'Remember when you were rushed to hospital with appendicitis? My precious little girl...' His fingers squeezed hers. 'Your mother rang me just before I went into court. You had peritonitis. You were fighting for your life. I wanted to drop everything and come to you straight away...'

'Why didn't you?' she whispered. If only he had! 'Why *didn't* you ask for an adjournment?'

He lifted his shoulders, and let them fall. 'Misguided professional pride...something like that. I had a reputation for never allowing my personal life to interfere with a case, or stop me from doing my job. Only I did let my feelings affect this particular case, didn't I?' His eyes glistened with emotion. 'And your friend Simon knew it—he was aware I should have taken a harder line, should have given more time to the case. I saw the way he looked at me when the verdict was brought down. The hate, the bitterness...'

Tanya said quickly, 'He doesn't feel that way now, Daddy. He says he's always found you to be a fine barrister—and a fine judge.'

'If he truly loves you,' her father said gruffly, 'he may understand why I wasn't functioning at my best that day, and find it in his heart to forgive me.'

She felt her heart squeeze with surprised relief. This was her father's way of acknowledging Simon's love for her—and giving it his sanction. Giving *Simon* his sanction.

'I'm sure he will, Daddy,' she whispered, hoping with all her heart that he would. And would forgive her too, for doubting him.

She wanted to call Simon there and then, but it was far too late. Besides, this was something they needed to talk over face to face, not over the phone. Tomorrow she would call his chambers and try to arrange a lunchtime meeting.

But her hopes were dashed when his secretary, Gail, told her that Simon had accepted a country brief, and was expected to be away for most of the week. No, she couldn't say where he was staying.

Couldn't? Or wouldn't? Tanya pondered in agonised suspense as she hung up. Had he gone away deliberately, to put distance between them, thinking it was all over between them? After all, she *had* sent him away!

No! She refused to believe that he could have turned his back on her for good. He had gone away simply to give her time to think things over. Everything would be all right once she'd had a chance to speak to him. *Wouldn't* it?

How on earth was she going to get through the week?

The days and nights dragged painfully by. She couldn't settle to anything, couldn't concentrate on her work, could barely eat, though she tried to hide her agony whenever Ellie was around. She didn't want to talk about it, even to Ellie.

On Thursday, she tried Simon's chambers again, but he still hadn't come back. His secretary suggested she try again the next afternoon—she expected to know his movements by then.

After a sleepless night and a blurred, interminably long morning at the office, Tanya nervously snatched up the phone.

'I'm sorry,' came the words she had been dreading for the past twenty-four hours. 'Mr Devlin has called in to say he won't be back in town this week...' Then, on a brighter note, 'He'll be going straight home to his property in Gippsland after his case finishes today...perhaps you can reach him there.'

Tanya thanked her and rang off, pressing her chest with repressed excitement. Simon would be at home, at his place in the bush, by this evening! She only had to drive up there and——

But would he want to see her? Her doubts flooded back. It might be wise if she didn't call him first. He might tell her not to come! Best if she simply arrived, unannounced.

But what if he had someone else with him? She groaned, refusing to believe that he would have turned to someone else so quickly. But if he thought that she had turned away from him for good...if he had been looking for consolation...

She thought of Dimity Donohue, panting to break down Simon's defences, and she squeezed her eyes shut, trying to blot out the picture that rose to her mind. All that mattered now was to get to him as quickly as she could and assure him that she still loved him, that nothing had changed. And then she would broach the matter of her father, and let him know that her father, who had never asked forgiveness of any man, was now begging for Simon's understanding over a mistake he had made seventeen-odd years ago, perhaps his only mistake in a long and distinguished career—a mistake he had made because he had been worried sick about *her*. If Simon loved her as much as her father did, surely he would understand why her father had been distracted that day, and make allowances?

She dashed home after work, flung a few things into an overnight bag, and left a note for Ellie telling her where she had gone.

It wasn't a good night for driving. Darkness was already closing in as she swung out into the road, the clouds were low and ominously dark, and a strong wind was buffeting the car, swirling dry leaves into the air and sending them scudding across the windscreen.

But she barely noticed. All that was really penetrating her consciousness at the moment was the thought of seeing Simon again, of setting things right between them.

If she could.

Simon would have had time to think too. He might have come to the bitter conclusion that their differences were insurmountable, not worth fighting to overcome. He had seen the way she had turned away from him. It must have looked to Simon as if she were putting her father before him, *her* world before his.

'No!' she cried aloud, startling herself. 'I don't care a damn where I live any more, so long as I'm with you, Simon! That's all that matters.'

A vivid flash of lightning made her blink, and almost at the same time a deafening clap of thunder split the skies. It was like a signal from above, coming, ironically, at the same instant as the truth struck her, as she realised for the first time how blind, how selfish she had been. All this time she had been thinking only of herself, hoping Simon would change his mind and decide to stay in town in *her* comfortable world. She had never once put herself into Simon's shoes and considered what *he* wanted, or where *he* needed to be. Always, she had been thinking of what would be easiest, most acceptable to herself!

The rain was tumbling down now, blurring the windscreen, and she realised she would have to start concentrating if she were to have any hope of finding the turn-off to Simon's place. She gave a hoot of triumph when she found it, confirming it moments later as she passed the warning sign she had noticed before: 'Kangaroos next 5K'. She wasn't too concerned about coming across a kangaroo or a wombat tonight—surely no animal would be wandering about in this storm! But she slowed down, just in case.

How lucky it was that she did. Next thing she knew, a dark bulk had loomed from nowhere, and as she slammed on the brakes, she heard a thud, and saw, in the beam of the headlights, a giant kangaroo hop away into the bush. She had only given the animal a glancing blow, thank God. But the car, she realised in dismay, had slewed sideways into the soft earth—mushy now after the rain—and when she tried to drive on, the rear wheel spun uselessly, churning up mud. After a few vain attempts to free the car, she knew that it was hopelessly bogged!

Damn! She flung open the door, cursing herself for not bringing a waterproof jacket—or even an umbrella. One look at the car and she knew that even if she managed to put something under the rear wheel, she would never be able to get the car out on her own. She needed help—someone to come and tow her out. She could wait for a car to come along, but she might have a long wait—and how did she know she could trust whoever came along? This was a pretty deserted road, and she was a female on her own.

No, there was no help for it. She would have to start walking—and hope that Simon's place wasn't too far away. Simon would help her.

If he was at home.

Through the booming cannon fire of the 1812 Overture and the reverberating rolls of thunder overhead, Simon was dimly conscious of a different kind of banging. He opened his eyes and frowned. Who on earth would be banging on his door at this time of night? Just when he'd settled down to listen to his new compact disc.

Not that he was giving it his full attention, so what the hell? Even the explosive cannon fire couldn't keep his mind fully focused on the music—his subconscious mind kept throwing up images of hurt violet-blue eyes and soft trembling lips, a stricken heart-shaped face in a silky mass of honey-blonde hair...

With a sigh he rose from his armchair, turned down the thunderous sounds of battle, and strode across the room. When he switched on the outside light and pulled open the front door, for a second he failed to recognise the pathetic, sodden creature on his doorstep.

The rain had darkened her hair and plastered it to her pale face, she had scratches on her cheeks and muddy streaks across her forehead, and the loose woollen sweater she was wearing hung shapelessly from her slim frame, over her soaked jeans. He saw her begin to sway as she bent to pull at her wet, muddy sneakers, and he reached out swiftly to support her.

'For pity's sake—*Tanya!* What's happened to you? Have you had an accident?' Anxiety roughened his voice.

Her frozen lips moved stiffly, curving slightly as she answered. 'Sort of. My car got bogged, way back along the road. *Miles* back. I had to walk. I feel as if I've been walking all night!'

'These scratches...' As Simon gently took her chin in one hand and tilted her face towards his, Tanya explained, 'A b-branch blew into my face.'

He put his arm round her and dragged her inside, into the blessed warmth and dryness of the quarry-tiled lobby.

'You walked all this way in the dark? In this storm? Didn't you have a coat in the car? An umbrella?' He was rubbing her arms, rubbing the circulation back into her veins, as he fired the questions at her.

She shook her head. 'I wasn't really planning on running into a kangaroo and getting bogged. It's all right,' she was quick to assure him, 'I saw him hop away. I didn't hurt him.'

Simon's hands had stilled on her arms, and his fingers were digging into her flesh. 'You were lucky he didn't hurt *you*!'

'I wasn't driving fast, luckily. I remembered your warning.'

'So calm! Can this be the girl who screams at spiders and jumps at noises in the night?' As she glanced up at him, she saw a return of the old mocking gleam to his eyes. And there was something else there too, that she couldn't read so easily.

'So I can rough it when I have to,' she said with a wobbly attempt at a grin. 'I don't always take the easy way out, you see? If I want something badly enough, I'll fight tooth and nail to get it.' Her teeth were chattering as she spoke, but her eyes were telling him loud and clear that what she had battled through tonight was nothing compared to what she was really fighting for.

'I always said you'd surprise me one day,' was the only comment Simon made, but there was a thickness in his voice that overrode the mockery and caused her to swallow hard. 'Did you leave your car locked? Is it off the road?' When she nodded he said, 'I'll pick it up in the morning. Here...' he burrowed into a cupboard and grabbed a fluffy towel '...let me dry your hair and then we'll get you into a hot shower—and see to those grazes.'

As he rubbed her hair, being careful not to brush the towel across her wounds, he asked, 'What possessed you to drive up here on your own on a night like tonight? Why didn't you let me know you were coming? I'd have come for you.'

With her head under the towel, her answer, when it came, was muffled. 'I—I wasn't sure you'd want to see me again...'

'Wouldn't *want*——!' He flicked the towel aside, his eyes blazing into hers. Tanya felt something catch in her throat when she saw that it was naked emotion, not anger, that blazed there. 'If you only knew what I've been going through this past week! Thinking you might never come back to me!'

'It's been agony for me too,' she whispered. 'Thinking I might have lost *you*. Let's never be parted again, Simon...p-promise?' By now her teeth were clicking like castanets.

'Promise.' He wrapped the towel gently round her head. Then he scooped her up in his powerful arms. 'Come on into that shower. We can talk afterwards.'

'Yes...we must. I have so much to tell you,' she whispered, wondering with a faint qualm how Simon would react to her father's agonised appeal. Would he be prepared to forgive and forget? Would he at least be understanding, sympathetic?

She was anxious to tell him too about her own change of heart, about her decision to make a new life with him out here in the bush. About that, she had no qualms whatsoever.

They sat wrapped in each other's arms in front of the open fire, their conversation at times smothered by feverish kisses and hungry embraces. Simon was quick to allay Tanya's worries on her father's behalf, assuring her with a melting tenderness in his eyes that he understood, that there was nothing to forgive, and that he was relieved to know that her father's distracted air on that long-ago day had been due to concern over his ailing daughter and had nothing whatever to do with any *lack* of concern for his brother Chris.

'In fact,' Simon admitted heavily, 'I've done your father a grave injustice, implying that he was biased against my brother, implying that he looked on Chris as a roughneck from the bush, a nobody who was hardly worth the effort. I'm glad I was wrong about that.'

Tanya chewed on her lip. 'I know my father can be an awful snob, but I don't think he's ever let his opinions carry over into the courtroom. When he was at the bar, he always took pride in the fact that he did the very best he could for each and every one of his clients—bad, good, rich or poor. It was only that one time...' Her voice broke, and she bowed her head.

'I guess we all have a weak spot—a human side,' Simon said quietly, running his fingers through her freshly washed hair, exulting in its silkiness, wondering with a lump in his throat how he might react if, during a court appearance, he heard that this woman he loved was hovering between life and death...

Tanya looked up at him, her eyes misty with unshed tears. 'My weak spot is you,' she confessed. 'I would follow you anywhere, Simon...I know that now. I just want to be with you. Now and forever... Oh, Simon, I've been such a fool,' she said, slipping her hand inside his shirt and letting it glide over his warm, smooth skin and tangle in the curly hair below his throat. 'I've been so selfish!'

He hushed her with a smiling, 'No, I've been the selfish one. Expecting you to come and live out here, expecting you to give up your job in town, and a lot more besides. Mm...keep doing that, I love it.' He kissed the tip of her nose. 'We'll go on just the way we are now...living and working in town. We'll come up here at weekends, whenever we can, and maybe we'll spend some of our holidays here. But that's it. If I find I need to, I can always hire a manager to look after the place.'

She was overcome by his generosity, by the sacrifice he was offering to make for her sake. But——

'No.' She heard the finality in her voice, and knew that she meant it. She slipped her hand round behind his back, and began stroking his spine with a feather-light touch. 'We'll live here and we'll run the property ourselves...and we'll think about starting up a small legal practice somewhere in the vicinity, so that we don't get rusty...and we'll bring up our children here...'

Their eyes met, and now there was a mistiness on both sides. 'What marvellous ideas you come up with,' he said, arching his back under the sensuous brush of her fingertips. 'That's delicious...don't stop.' His own hands were doing some subtle exploring of their own—one was resting at the nape of her neck, the circular motion of his thumbtip sending exquisite shivers down her spine, while his other hand had found its way inside the robe she had borrowed from him, and was gently massaging her bare midriff, causing tiny shock waves to throb through her.

'Do you mean it?' he said huskily. 'That's really what you want?'

'It's really what I want.' Tanya gasped as his hand moved even lower. This was exquisite torture! 'As long as you're with me, of course.'

'I'll be with you all right... Oh, Tanya, I can't stand this any longer.' He buried his face in the silken valley between her breasts.

An instant flame leapt between them and it was a long time before either of them uttered another coherent word.

The most telling words of all came the following morning when Tanya stood at the long windows gazing out over the emerald green hills, watching the sunlight glistening on the wet leaves of Simon's beloved trees. With an ecstatic sigh, she turned to Simon and, with all her love shining from her eyes, whispered contentedly, 'I feel as if I've come home.'

'You *are* home,' said Simon, and in one stride, he had her in his arms, where she belonged.

Coming soon
to an easy chair near you.

FIRST CLASS is Harlequin's armchair travel plan for the incurably romantic. You'll visit a different dreamy destination every month from January through December without ever packing a bag. No jet lag, no expensive air fares and *no* lost luggage. Just First Class Harlequin Romance reading, featuring exotic settings from Tasmania to Thailand, from Egypt to Australia, and more.

FIRST CLASS romantic excursions guaranteed! Start your world tour in January. Look for the special **FIRST CLASS** destination on selected Harlequin Romance titles—there's a new one every month.

NEXT DESTINATION:
GREECE

 Harlequin Books

JTR4

Harlequin Intrigue®

A SPAULDING & DARIEN MYSTERY
by Robin Francis

An engaging pair of amateur sleuths—Jenny Spaulding and Peter Darien—were introduced to Harlequin Intrigue readers in #147, BUTTON, BUTTON (Oct. 1990). Jenny and Peter will return for further spine-chilling romantic adventures in April 1991 in #159, DOUBLE DARE in which they solve their next puzzling mystery. Two other books featuring Jenny and Peter will follow in the A SPAULDING AND DARIEN MYSTERY series.

HARLEQUIN
Romance®

Coming Next Month

#3115 ARROGANT INVADER Jenny Arden
There had never been much love lost between Gwenyth Morgan and
Jeb Hunter, though now he seems determined to pursue her. But since
Gwenyth is happily engaged to Marc and planning a future in France, what is
there to be afraid of?

#3116 LOVE'S AWAKENING Rachel Ford
Just sixteen when she'd been emotionally blackmailed into marrying
Alex Petrides, Selina had run away within hours of the wedding. Alex hadn't
followed as she'd expected. Now, three years later, something irresistibly
draws her back to Greece.

#3117 THE ONLY MAN Rosemary Hammond
Her father's death and her fiancé's jilting leaves Jennie in shock. Then
Alex Knight, her father's friend, gives her a home and a job at his winery. But
Alex treats her as a child when Jennie longs to be recognized as a woman....

#3118 TWO AGAINST LOVE Ellen James
Christie Daniels has just managed to escape one domineering man—her
father—when she's confronted with another. Matt Gallagher's mission is to
talk her into leaving her New Mexico bed-and-breakfast and returning to her
father's brokerage firm in New York City. Christie has no intention of
agreeing, but she *does* wish Matt weren't so darned attractive....

#3119 AN UNCOMMON AFFAIR Leigh Michaels
Marsh Endicott mistakenly thinks Torey Farrell will be pleased to sell him her
half share of the house they jointly inherited. Torey, though, can't wait to
start a new life in the house—and certainly doesn't want a ready-made,
already engaged housemate!

#3120 RITES OF LOVE Rebecca Winters
Courtney Blake, who's half Miccosukee, accuses the man she loves of
betraying the tribe's faith in him. She flees to her mother's family in the
Everglades, but Jonas follows her—and forces her to confront her own lack of
faith in their love.

Available in April wherever paperback books are sold, or through
Harlequin Reader Service:

In the U.S.
P.O. Box 1397
Buffalo, N.Y.
14240-1397

In Canada
P.O. Box 603
Fort Erie, Ontario
L2A 5X3